ESCAPE *into the* NIGHT

FREEDOM 1 SEEKERS

ESCAPE *into the* NIGHT

LOIS WALFRID JOHNSON

MOODY PUBLISHERS

CHICAGO

Previously published as The Riverboat Adventures Series

Scripture quotations are from the King James Version of the Bible.

Interior Design: Ragont Design
Side-wheeler illustration by Toni Auble
Map of Upper Mississippi by Meridian Mapping
Cover Design: Brock, Sharp & Associates / Faceout Studio
Cover Image: Odessa Sawyer

978-0-8024-0716-0 - Printed by Bethany Press in Bloomington, MN – 02/13

Library of Congress Cataloging-in-Publication Data

Johnson, Lois Walfrid. The Freedom Seekers
  Escape into the night / Lois Walfrid Johnson.
     p.   cm. — (The freedom seekers ; #1)
  Summary: In 1857 thirteen-year-old Libby joins her father aboard the *Christina* and proves that she can be trusted to assist in the escape of a fugitive slave.
    ISBN 978-0-8024-0716-0
  [1. Fugitive slaves—Fiction. 2. Slavery—Fiction. 3. Afro-Americans—Fiction.]
  I. Title. II. Series: Johnson, Lois Walfrid. The Freedom Seekers; #1
  PZ7.J63255Es   1995
  [Fic]—dc20   95–18990
  ISBN 978-0-80240716-0   CIP
                          AC

We hope you enjoy this book from Moody Publishers. Our goal is to provide high-quality, thought-provoking books and products that connect truth to your real needs and challenges. For more information on other books and products written and produced from a biblical perspective, go to www.moodypublishers.com or write to:

Moody Publishers
820 N. LaSalle Boulevard
Chicago, IL 60610

1 3 5 7 9 10 8 6 4 2

Printed in the United States of America

To each of you who have told me
how much you like
the Adventures of the Northwoods
and Viking Quest books
I dedicate this
Freedom Seekers series
to you.
Love always!

* * * * * * * *

Elijah Lovejoy, Dr. and Mrs. William Salter, Henderson Lewelling, Amos and Ellen Kimberly and their son Samuel, Reverend Asa Turner, and Deacon and Mrs. Theron Trowbridge are all historic characters who lived in the 1850s. Emma is based on the story of a real mother helped by Deacon Trowbridge. All other characters are fictitious and spring with gratitude for life from the author's imagination. Any resemblance to persons living or dead is coincidental.

In the time in which this book is set,
African Americans were called *Negro*,
the Spanish word for black,
or colored people.

Contents

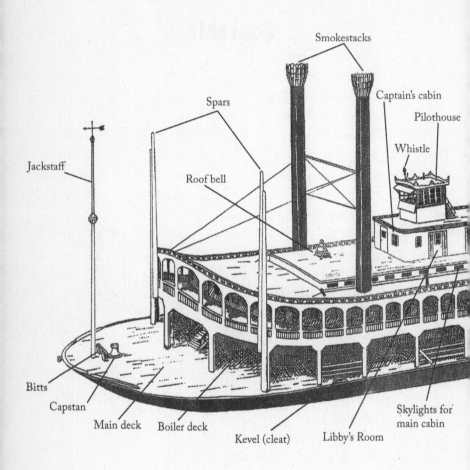

Smokestacks

Spars

Captain's cabin

Pilothouse

Whistle

Jackstaff

Roof bell

Bitts

Capstan

Main deck

Boiler deck

Kevel (cleat)

Libby's Room

Skylights for
main cabin

The Side-Wheeler
Christina

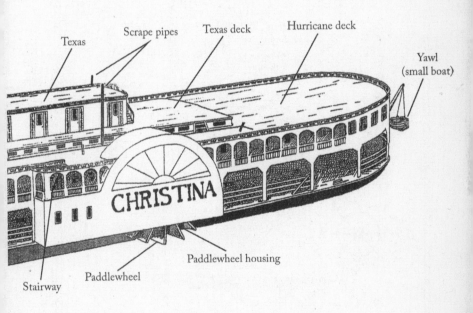

Texas   Scrape pipes   Texas deck   Hurricane deck

Yawl
(small boat)

CHRISTINA

Paddlewheel housing

Stairway   Paddlewheel

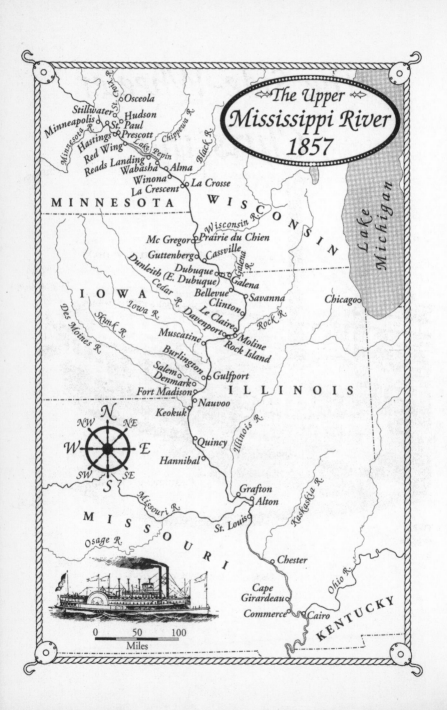

CHAPTER 1

Nighttime Surprises

A slender moon hung in the night sky as Libby Norstad gazed down from the hotel. In the river below, her father's steamboat lay next to the landing. Dark now except for a lantern near the gangplank, the *Christina* seemed to be asleep.

Then as Libby's eyes grew used to the darkness, a shadow separated from a building off to the right. A second shadow followed, and a third. Without making a sound, three men crept toward the river.

At a warehouse near the *Christina* they stopped. As silently as they came, the men crept around the building and disappeared.

A few minutes later the three men returned. This time they slipped into the deep shadows next to the warehouse. All during that March day in 1857 it had rained, and a large puddle lay between the tall building and the steamboat.

Trying to catch even one small movement, Libby peered into the night. Soon clouds blotted out what little moon there was, making it even more difficult to see.

Just then Libby heard voices from the sitting room next door. Her father was there, and her aunt. Libby strained to hear.

"She's thirteen now. She needs a change in her life." That was Pa, and Libby knew he was talking about her. But the rest of his words faded away.

Without making a sound, Libby slipped over to another window. There she was closer to the wall between her bedroom and the sitting room.

"Somehow that girl always manages to attract trouble!" That was Auntie Vi speaking.

Libby pressed her ear against the wall. At the same time she stared down at the warehouse. Not one movement gave away the three men.

Then from somewhere in the night a dog barked. In the next instant the men leaped from the shadows. Breaking into a run, they headed straight for the large puddle between them and the *Christina*. Long boards lay across the puddle, but the men sloshed through the water with bare feet.

In the same moment a boy raced across the *Christina's* deck. When he reached the oil lantern, he blew out the flame. Sudden darkness hid the men.

Libby raised the window and leaned forward, straining to see. What had happened to the men? She felt sure they were trying to board her father's boat.

As Libby wondered if she should warn him, the quiet night seemed to explode. Around the hotel the streets came alive. Instead of one dog barking, there were several.

Soon Libby heard dogs enter the street just below her window. Eight or ten men ran close behind with lanterns held high. In their light Libby saw leaping dogs. Yipping with excitement, they strained at their leashes. Bloodhounds!

The dogs sniffed along the side of the warehouse, then followed the trail to the large puddle of water. At first the lead dog sniffed his way onto the boards. Seeming to find no scent, he went back to the edge of the puddle. This time he sniffed his way around it.

On the far side, the bloodhound barked again. As the other dogs joined him, their barking set up howls from dogs all over town.

Nose to the ground, the lead dog sniffed his way toward the *Christina*. At the edge of the riverbank he stopped. Looking up at the tall, heavy man who held his leash, the dog barked.

"Hey there!" the large man shouted. "You on the *Christina*!"

As the man held up his lantern, Libby saw that something had changed. The long plank from boat to shore was no longer in place.

When no one appeared, the man shouted again. "Hey there! I know you're on board! C'mon out!"

Around him, the dogs set up an even greater racket. Then a lantern moved slowly across the forward deck. When the person with the lantern held it up, Libby recognized the boy she had seen only minutes before.

From near the railing he called down. "Can I help you?"

"Of course you can help me! Where are the men that boarded your boat?"

"You saw men?" the boy asked.

"Where is your captain?" the large man roared.

"He'll be back soon, sir. Would you like to wait?"

"Where's your first mate?"

"I can't tell you, sir."

"Then let us board!"

"I can't let you board, sir. Not without the captain's permission."

"Then run out your gangplank! We'll tell you whether someone went aboard!"

The boy stepped backward and set down the lantern. As Libby watched, a long plank dropped down between the boat and the shore.

Once again the boy held up the lantern, but he stayed at the top of the gangplank. Strong and confident looking, he guarded the deck, as though unwilling to let anyone step past him.

With the lead dog running ahead, the pack of dogs pushed forward. Nose to the wood, he sniffed up and down the plank. Finally he returned to his owner and sat down on his haunches.

Holding up his fist, the large man shook it at the boy on board. "I don't know what you did!"

The boy seemed undisturbed. "Maybe you should look somewhere else," he called down.

The man's sudden growl sounded like a dog's. Just the same, he turned away. When the bloodhounds sniffed their way back to the warehouse, the men followed.

As they disappeared around the end of the building, Libby heard voices in the sitting room. Quickly she tiptoed across the floor and knelt down at the door between the two rooms.

"I just can't seem to change Libby into what she should be." That was Auntie Vi again.

Since the death of her mother four years before, Libby had lived with her aunt and uncle in a Chicago mansion. In that second week of March 1857, Libby and Auntie Vi had traveled to Burlington, Iowa, so that Libby could visit her father.

"How do you want to change her?" Captain Norstad asked.

"She can't do *anything* right!" Auntie Vi answered. "She does like nice clothes, but—"

"She likes nice clothes, all right!" the captain agreed. "Libby told me that she didn't like my uniform—that it's too old-fashioned!"

"That sounds like Libby." Her aunt sounded pleased. "She's developed excellent taste. Whatever costs most, that's what Libby chooses."

"Does she now?" the captain asked. "Is that why she calls me *Faw-thur*, like some high society girl? The last time I saw Libby I was her pa."

Trying to catch every word, Libby leaned closer. She'd have to remember to call her father Pa. In the darkness she bumped against the door. Scared by the light thud, she drew back. Had her aunt and father heard?

When they went on talking, Libby knew she was safe. Once more she put her ear to the keyhole.

"So what exactly is the problem?" Captain Norstad asked.

"Though she likes nice things, Libby acts like a tomboy. I was horrified when I caught her swimming! A proper young lady would never swim."

"Unless her father showed her how." Captain Norstad's voice sounded dangerously low. "I taught Libby to swim, in case she fell off my boat."

"But she embarrasses me in front of my friends!" Auntie Vi wailed. "I'm ready to give up on that girl!"

Give up on me? As though a knife pierced her heart, Libby felt the pain of those words. *Auntie Vi wants to give up on me?*

"Well, *I'm* not ready to give up," the captain answered. "I'll *never* give up on Libby!"

But Libby barely heard her father's words. So upset that she forgot to be quiet, she again bumped against the door.

In the next instant Libby heard quick footsteps moving toward her. As she scrambled to get away, the door opened. Her father reached out and took her hand.

"We need to talk about something." He drew her into the sitting room. "Sit down, Libby."

"I want to stand, sir." Whatever her punishment would be, Libby knew she couldn't take it sitting down. "If you please, sir," she added quickly.

Auntie Vi sat in a chair near the fireplace. In the lamplight Libby saw her aunt's eyes. She was not happy with the way things were going.

As though walking the deck of a steamboat, Captain Norstad took a turn around the room. Libby remembered what that meant. Her father had something important to say.

When he reached a window on the front side of the hotel, the captain paused. Holding aside the curtain, he looked down.

Did he see the men and dogs? Libby wondered as the curtain fell back over the window.

Then her father turned to her. With his black hair and captain's uniform, he looked tall and distinguished. "Libby, I've made up my mind. I want you to live on the *Christina* with me."

Libby's heart leaped. *I'll be with my father—my pa—again!* Never in her wildest imagination had she thought he would allow that.

But her aunt broke in. "A girl Libby's age without her mother on a riverboat? That's unthinkable!"

"Is it?" Captain Norstad asked. "Libby and I barely know each other anymore. I want to be part of her life, to help her grow up. I get lonesome for her."

Pa is lonesome for me? Libby felt glad. More than once since the death of her mother, she had cried herself to sleep. She had felt lonely for both parents.

"It's not safe for Libby to live on your boat!" Auntie Vi exclaimed.

"It wasn't safe when she was eight or nine, but Libby is thirteen now. I'll get her a dog."

"A dog?" Libby asked, startled. She wasn't sure about that. She'd seen a lot of dogs running around the streets of Chicago. Dogs that were dirty and mean and got into fights. "Are you sure I need a dog?"

"He'll protect you."

Suddenly Libby remembered something else. "I don't have enough clothes along. How can I possibly live with only one trunkful?"

"You'll manage!" Pa's voice was gruff now, and Libby knew that no one would change his mind. For good or bad, she would live on the *Christina.*

Like a giant wave, the idea washed over her. Libby felt excited, but also scared. Often she'd heard people talk about the dangerous things that happened to steamboats. They exploded or caught fire. They struck the hidden roots of old trees and sank within minutes. Gamblers traveled on the boats—and thieves.

Whenever she heard those stories, Libby had worried

about her father. Now, living on the *Christina*, she would share that danger.

Then she remembered her aunt's words—words that hurt all the way through. Standing tall, Libby faced her father. "If I live on the *Christina*, I want a never-give-up family."

"What do you mean, Libby?" he asked.

Libby looked straight into his eyes. "I want a family that believes in me, even when I'm not perfect."

A sob rose in her throat, but Libby kept on. "A family that sticks together, even though it's hard."

Tears welled up in her eyes. Unwilling to have her aunt see her cry, Libby tried to blink back her tears. Instead they spilled over.

"That's the kind of family I want too," Pa said softly. "We can be that family for each other."

"With just two people?"

Pa nodded. "If we don't give up on each other."

Libby found it hard to believe. "You might not like how I act."

"You might not like what I ask you to do," Pa answered.

"But we can practice," Libby said.

"We'll practice hard." Her father had a twinkle in his eye. "Caleb and the other people who work on the *Christina* will be our larger family."

Captain Norstad glanced toward Auntie Vi. "I need to leave Burlington tomorrow."

"Tomorrow?" Libby asked. This time her scared feelings went right down to her toes. *What will my new life be like?*

~ CHAPTER 2 ~

The Mysterious Boxes

The next morning, standing outside the hotel where she and Auntie Vi had spent the night, Libby felt a tingle of excitement. *I'm beginning my new life! I wonder what adventures I'll have!*

Of all the steamboats at the landing, her father's paddleboat seemed the most beautiful. Even now, smoke billowed from the tall stacks. In the sunlight the railings and pilothouse shone.

Then Auntie Vi joined Libby, and they started down the street to the river. Libby studied the name on the wooden housing of the great side paddlewheel.

"*Christina* for my ma," she said. The four-deck-high steamboat was a proud reminder of the mother Libby still loved with all her heart.

"Christina was a red-haired beauty," Auntie Vi answered. She and Libby's mother had been sisters. "Deep red hair with gold highlights—the same color as yours. Same brown eyes too. Men for miles around wanted to marry her—"

"I know, I know," Libby broke in. She had heard the story at least a hundred times.

"Your mother could have married any wealthy man she chose," Auntie went on. "Why she picked your father I'll never know!"

Libby searched the sky behind the *Christina*. She felt as if a cloud had passed over the sun. To her surprise it still shone.

"Ma married Pa because she loved him." Libby's voice sounded sharp, even to her own ears. "And I love him too!"

"Love never pays the bills," her aunt answered, as she always did. "If you find living on the boat too hard, your Uncle Alex and I will welcome you home."

Libby didn't want to think about returning to her aunt's. Not now, anyway, when she looked forward to her new life. Instead, Libby remembered her aunt's hurtful words. *She thinks I'm not worth anything. Maybe she's right.*

Trying to push aside her nervousness, Libby slipped her hand between the folds of her full skirt. The white cloth of her new dress felt soft to her touch. With a toss of her head Libby set her face toward the *Christina*.

This is the first day of my new life! I won't let anyone spoil it!

Picking up her pace, Libby walked as fast as she dared. In one more hour her aunt would go back to Chicago. *I only need to get through the next hour.*

Just then Libby hiccuped.

"Child!" her aunt exclaimed. "How can you get hiccups at a time like this?"

"I don't know." Libby wished she could push aside her nervousness. Not since she was nine years old had she been on a steamboat. In the midst of her next hiccup Libby swallowed hard.

Her aunt glared at her. "Breathe deep, and they'll stop."

As they reached the landing, Libby took a deep breath. Her father waited at the top of the gangplank, looking tall and handsome. Two men dressed in black suits, stiff white shirts, and bow ties stood next to him.

Auntie Vi stopped Libby. "Remember now," she said. "I've brought you up to be a proper young lady."

"Yes, Auntie." Libby hiccuped. "I'll do my best."

"Hold your breath!" her aunt exclaimed.

All the way up the gangplank Libby held her breath. At the top her father stretched out his hand.

"Welcome aboard, Libby!" He put his arm around her. "I'm glad we'll be together again."

Captain Norstad turned to the officers next to him. "This is the very special daughter I've been telling you about."

Libby tried to smile, but she needed to breathe. "I'm glad to meet you," she said quickly. Her words ended in a loud hiccup.

Libby clapped her hands over her mouth. She wanted to run and hide. "I'm sorry," she apologized. Again she held her breath, this time so long that she felt like fainting. *How can I embarrass my father so?*

"Libby, stop it!" her aunt commanded. But Libby gasped with another great hiccup.

"We'll get you a glass of water." Captain Norstad sounded as if it wasn't at all unusual to have his family hiccup in front of his officers. "This is Mr. Osborne, the *Christina*'s chief engineer."

Afraid to open her mouth, Libby nodded.

"And Mr. Bates, my first mate."

Mr. Bates was almost as tall as her father. When Libby hiccuped yet again, he pressed his thin lips together in a frown. It wasn't hard to tell what he thought of her.

By now a mask had settled over Auntie's face. From long experience Libby knew that she had shamed her aunt. But Captain Norstad didn't seem to notice.

"I'll show you Libby's room," he told Auntie Vi, as though nothing had happened. "You'll feel better if you see how I plan to take care of her."

He led them toward the wide stairs at the front of the steamboat. Libby hurried after him. The sooner they finished this, the quicker Auntie would be on her way.

The second level, or boiler deck, was above the large boilers that heated water and created steam to run the boat. Here Captain Norstad led Libby and her aunt through a large door.

A long, narrow room—the main cabin—stretched from one end of the boat to another. Waiters in white coats moved about, setting the tables for lunch. Her father asked one of the men for a glass of water for Libby. As though she hadn't had a sip in months, Libby swallowed the water in one gulp.

Outside the cabin again, Captain Norstad led them up another stairway. When they reached the hurricane deck, Libby walked over to the Burlington side of the boat. Directly below lay the landing. Beyond that was the warehouse where the three men had crept last night.

Again Libby wondered if her father had seen the running men and sniffing dogs. If he had, he gave no sign.

Just then Libby noticed that her aunt was out of breath. "Pa," she said quickly. "Auntie looks white."

Though Vi gasped for air, she held up her hand. "I'm fine— just fine."

From inside her sleeve, Auntie Vi pulled a lace handkerchief. As though using her last ounce of strength, she blotted her perspiring forehead.

But Libby knew what was wrong. To look thin and fashionable, Auntie laced her undergarments so tight that she couldn't breathe.

When Captain Norstad offered his arm, Auntie Vi took it. Walking slowly, he led her up the few steps to the texas deck. Named after the state recently added to the Union, the boxlike structure held rooms for some of the crew.

Captain Norstad had the best place of all—an apartment at the front of the texas. From the windows on the front and two sides of the boat, he could see everything that went on.

Above this room was the pilothouse, but Libby knew her father wouldn't take Auntie Vi up another flight of steps. Instead, he led her and Libby to the stateroom behind his.

As Captain Norstad opened the door, Mr. Bates hurried out. In both arms he carried clothes and blankets. As he glanced toward Libby, he scowled.

Strange, Libby thought. *I just met him, but he doesn't like me. I wonder why.*

Moments later she found out.

"I gave you the first mate's room," her father said. "I want you next to me."

So I get the second-best room on the boat, Libby told herself and felt glad.

After one peek through the window of Libby's room, her aunt turned away. In spite of the coolness of the March day, she glanced up at the sun.

"Why don't you look around?" Captain Norstad told Libby. "I'll take Vi down to the main deck."

By now Auntie's face had changed from white to red. Bringing out a small fan, she waved it back and forth.

Grateful to be alone, Libby walked into her stateroom.

About seven or eight feet wide and six feet long, it had one bed and a few coat hooks. Beneath a mirror, a small stand held a basin, a water pitcher, and a chamber pot.

From this place I'll see the world! Libby's excitement returned.

But as Libby turned around, her full skirt filled the entire area between her bed and the washstand. Where will I put my trunk? she wondered.

In Chicago Libby had lived in a mansion. Here, two doors led out of the tiny room, one on either side of the boat. Between those doors, the walls seemed to close in on Libby. *I could fit three of these rooms into my big room. And Auntie Vi always gave me whatever I wanted!*

Feeling she couldn't handle the small, narrow space, Libby rushed out. Like a chipmunk running for cover, she scurried into her father's cabin. Just looking at the larger room where he lived and worked made her feel better. At least she could turn around without her skirt touching something!

For a few minutes she stood there, drawing deep breaths. Not for anything would Libby admit how scared she felt. Scared of leaving her beautiful belongings in Chicago. Scared of all the changes in her life. Scared, most of all, by one thought. *People say it's really dangerous living on a steamboat!*

A short blast of the whistle broke into her thoughts. The signal for leaving Burlington! Libby yanked open the door.

When she hurried outside, she crashed into a boy. As a pail flew from his hand, water covered Libby from head to foot.

In horror she looked down. Dirty streaks of water covered her new white dress. More water dripped from her face.

"Why don't you watch where you're going?" she sputtered.

"Why don't *you* watch where *you're* going?" The boy's

blond hair fell over his forehead. Libby guessed that they were almost the same age.

Now his blue eyes glared at her. "What are you doing, snooping around here, anyway? That's the captain's room—off limits if you aren't invited!"

Libby straightened. She was almost the same height as this good-looking boy. "I have a perfect right to be here," she answered proudly. "I am Libby Norstad, the captain's daughter."

The boy stepped back in surprise. A red flush spread across his face.

Lifting her head, Libby tossed her long curls. "And who are you?"

"Caleb Whitney," he told her. "Your father's cabin boy." He spoke politely, but the anger did not leave his eyes. "I beg your pardon," he added, as though knowing he had no choice.

"I should hope so." With all the dignity Libby could manage, she started away. But suddenly she hiccuped.

When Caleb snickered, Libby felt even more embarrassed. Then she knew what to do. Her head still high, she turned around. "I'll speak to my father about you."

Caleb's grin faded. Standing with shoulders back, he answered, "Yes, miss." But his voice didn't sound as polite as his words.

Afraid she would hiccup again, Libby turned away and swept down the steps. Not until she reached the boiler deck did she remember.

With a shock she realized who the boy was. Last night she had seen him twice—both times on the main deck of the *Christina*.

Again she wondered what had happened to the men she

saw. "I'll ask Caleb," Libby decided. "He works for Pa. He'll have to tell me."

By the time she reached the main deck, the *Christina* had left Burlington. Libby found her father and aunt standing at the bow of the boat. Already the strip of water between boat and land had grown wide.

"Libby!" her aunt exclaimed. "Whatever happened to you?"

"I bumped into—" Libby started to put the blame on Caleb. Then she saw that her father was listening. His lips twitched, as if he wanted to laugh.

Libby didn't know what to do. *If I tell on Caleb, will he tell me about last night?*

In that instant she changed her words. "I came to say goodbye," Libby said instead.

Across the river from Burlington, Iowa, lay Gulfport, Illinois. As the *Christina* nosed into the landing, Libby saw railroad tracks and a waiting train.

"Don't forget," Auntie Vi told Libby. "You always have a home with us."

"I know," Libby answered softly. "Thanks for all you've done for me." As she leaned forward to kiss her aunt's cheek, Libby felt surprised at how hard it was to say goodbye. *Just because I'm scared! Just because Auntie's house seems so safe!*

Again the strange world along the Mississippi River seemed frightening. Yet Libby put on her best smile. Not for anything would she let Auntie know she had second thoughts about living on a steamboat.

Captain Norstad led Auntie Vi toward the train. From the bow of the *Christina*, Libby waved as if she didn't have a care in the world.

When the passengers had cleared the gangplank, deck-hands started carrying barrels and crates. Two men slid a large wooden box across the deck. With each man taking a side, they picked up the box and carried it down the gangplank. As they set it in a wagon on the landing, the boy Libby had met came down the steps.

By the time the deckhands returned to the boat, Caleb had taken up a post near the gangplank. Slender and self-assured, he wore the white coat and black trousers of a cabin boy.

"Careful, careful," he told the men as they picked up a second large box.

This one also seemed heavy. But it was Caleb who made Libby curious. Why was a cabin boy watching over the loading of freight?

In no time at all, the men had loaded the second box onto the wagon. As they slid a third box across the deck, the morning sun slanted against one side. The sun's rays lit a large knot-hole in the wood.

Suddenly Libby grew watchful. *Did something move inside that box? Or was it my imagination?*

Again Caleb guided the deckhands. Whatever the box held, it was both heavy and valuable.

When the men drew close to the railing, they picked up the box. With the weight balanced between them, one man backed toward the gangplank. Suddenly he stumbled over a small barrel.

Losing his grip, he tumbled backward. As the box crashed to the deck, Libby heard a groan.

Wanting to see more, she hurried forward. Just as quickly, Caleb stepped between her and the box.

CHAPTER 3

Here Comes Samson!

When Libby tried to walk around Caleb, he stopped her. "What do you think you're doing?" he asked.

Libby tossed her red curls. "I want to see what's going on."

"You're in the way," Caleb answered. "Please step aside. We need to put that box on the train."

For the second time in an hour, Libby looked down her nose. "And who do you think you are that I should listen to you? A cabin boy, no less! Trying to order me around!"

A flush of embarrassment reddened Caleb's face. But when Libby again tried to look at the knothole, he guarded the way.

"You take a lot of responsibility," she said.

"When Captain Norstad gives it to me, I take it," he answered.

Once more the two deckhands lifted the box between them. Walking carefully, they started down the gangplank.

This time Libby managed to slip around Caleb and follow. When the men reached the landing, they shoved the box onto the wagon. Caleb was right behind them.

"Go ahead!" he called to the driver.

As the team of horses started toward the train, the two

men jumped onto the end of the wagon. Libby walked along-side. Again Caleb followed her. "What are you doing, Libby Norstad?" he asked.

Libby pretended that she didn't hear him. The knothole in the wood no longer showed. That meant it had to be on the bottom side of the box. As Libby moved closer, she listened, but heard no other sound.

Caleb fell into step beside her. "What makes you so snoopy?" he asked.

"I want to know why those men have a box that says THIS SIDE UP resting on its side."

With a sweep of his hand Caleb pushed his hair out of his eyes. "You sure have a lot of curiosity. Does your father know you left the boat?"

"What does that have to do with the box?" Libby asked.

"We're putting out in a few minutes. He won't like it if we leave you behind."

"You're just saying that!"

"No, I'm not!"

Gongs from the ship's bell broke into Caleb's words. It was a signal for departure, Libby knew. But she couldn't remember the way the signal worked.

Having no choice but to believe Caleb, Libby stopped. Yet her gaze still followed the wagon and its strange cargo.

"I heard a sound," she said.

"You did?" Caleb stopped alongside Libby.

"A groan. A man's groan. I'm sure of it!"

"You are?" Caleb also watched the boxes.

Next to the open door of a freight car the driver stopped the wagon. The deckhands lifted the three boxes one by one and set them inside the car. When the last box was safely loaded, Caleb turned and started back to the *Christina*.

"There was a knothole," Libby said as she walked beside him. "Through the knothole I saw something move."

"That's odd." Caleb walked faster now, as if in a hurry to reach the boat. "What could be moving inside a box?"

"I told you!" Libby was growing impatient with him. "There's a man in the third box!"

"It's pretty hard to know whether it's a man if all you saw was a knothole."

"Caleb Whitney!" Libby stopped, unwilling to go another step. "It isn't just what I saw. It's also what I heard. If you had a brain in your head, you'd know that!"

As if ready to answer Libby, Caleb raised his chin. Instead, he glanced beyond her. Libby turned, curious about what he was seeing.

A short distance away, the first mate stood on the deck of the *Christina*. Libby felt sure he had been watching them. Mr. Bates even leaned slightly forward, as if straining to listen. Why did he want to hear what they said?

When Caleb spoke again, he seemed to have forgotten their disagreement. "You better hurry. Your father will wonder where you are."

This time Libby did not argue. Yet as she hurried up the gangplank, she gave one parting shot. "You are the strangest boy I ever met!"

When Caleb grinned, it surprised Libby. *He acts as if he's gotten his way.* But Libby didn't understand why.

~

In spite of Caleb's hurry, the *Christina* didn't leave port right away. As Libby and Caleb stood at the bow of the boat, he gazed toward the streets of Gulfport. "Your father's late."

Turning around, Libby looked up to the pilothouse perched on top of the texas. Even from here, she could see the upper part of the large wheel that steered the steamboat. Behind it stood the pilot, ready to guide the *Christina* out of port.

Libby's father was also licensed to pilot the boat. As captain and owner of the *Christina*, he spent most of his time taking care of business. Yet passengers liked to see him. When they came on board, his warm welcome gave them confidence in the safety of the boat.

As the bell gonged again, Caleb pointed toward the street. "There he is!"

With long strides Captain Norstad hurried toward the *Christina*. Next to him was something that looked like a great black bear.

Libby's heart sank. "A dog? A monstrous dog?"

"Your father got a Newfie!" Caleb exclaimed.

"A Newfie?" Libby hadn't wanted a dog in the first place, and this was the biggest one she had ever seen. "What's a Newfie?"

"Don't you know about Newfoundlands?" Caleb asked. "They're draft dogs."

"And what is a draft dog?"

"A working dog. For hundreds of years Newfies have pulled carts for their owners."

"You mean they work in harness like a horse?"

"They use harnesses, but no reins," Caleb told her. "They're trained to respond to voice commands."

Here, too, on this side of the river, mud puddles filled

the street. Captain Norstad stepped around them, but the dog didn't. While staying at the captain's side, the dog passed through every puddle, as if he enjoyed getting wet. Then his wet paws padded across the black dirt on the riverbank.

Nearby, steamboats buzzed with activity, but Libby had eyes for only one thing—that terrible dog. She had no doubt as to who would be taking care of it.

Seeing Libby, her father waved to her. "I found just what I wanted for you!"

As though catching the captain's excitement, the dog broke away. With quick bounds he raced up the gangplank, straight toward Libby. Leaping up, he planted his front paws on her shoulders.

Libby staggered back, almost falling over. She tried to push the dog away.

"Off!" the captain commanded, and the dog dropped to the deck.

But Libby still felt frightened. Then she looked down, and her scared feelings changed to anger. The dog had left great black patches of dirt on her already wet dress.

Sitting on his haunches, the monster stared up at Libby. Except for white patches on his chest and toes, he was completely black. His long tongue reached out, as if to say hello. But Libby wanted nothing to do with the dog.

"What's his name?" Already Caleb was down on his knees petting the dog.

So it's a boy, not a girl, Libby thought.

"Samson," her father said.

"Samson!" Libby exclaimed. "He's so big, he looks like *trouble!*"

"He's not." Her father's wide grin told Libby how pleased he felt. "Samson's a good dog. He just got carried away."

But Libby shared none of his excitement. "How did you find him so fast?"

"The last time I was in port I met his owners. They've taken good care of him. I'm glad Samson was still available."

Reaching out, the captain scratched behind the dog's ears. Samson wagged his tail as though the two were already friends.

"Look at his coat!" Caleb stroked the dog's back. "Nice and shiny, the way it should be. Not a burr in it!"

When he lifted the dog's great front paw, Caleb found a small stone caught between the webbed toes. As he brushed the stone away, Samson's tongue reached out to lick Caleb's face.

"I bought Samson for you, Libby," the captain said. "I want you to keep him with you."

Libby remembered her father's talk with Auntie Vi. "This dog is supposed to be my protector?" It seemed ridiculous after the way he almost knocked her over.

Libby's father smiled. "God is your real protector, but maybe Samson will help. He'll be good company for you."

"Good company!" Libby disliked even the idea. "I don't want a dog!"

"He can stay in your room."

"No!" The word exploded from Libby's lips. "I don't want this big dog in my little room!"

From his large, square-looking head, Samson gazed up at Libby as though he wanted to be friends. His brown eyes pleaded with her.

For a moment Libby felt sorry for the way she had spoken. She almost felt drawn to the dog. Then she pushed the idea away. Who wanted a four-legged friend who drooled and slurped all over your face if you got too close?

"Samson's a rescue dog," Caleb said quickly. "If a sailor falls into the sea, a Newfie goes after him."

"Well, there's no sea around here!"

"There's a river," Caleb was quick to point out.

"If you ever fell overboard, he'd rescue you," her father said.

"He would jump in after me?" For the first time Libby looked at Samson with respect.

The dog seemed to sense the change in Libby. Coming to his feet, he lifted one great paw, as though to say hello.

Looking down, Libby once more saw the dirt on her new dress. The white cloth would never again be the same.

Unable to bear the thought of caring for such a dog, Libby ran for the stairs. Partway up, she glanced back.

Near the bow of the *Christina*, Caleb stood next to Captain Norstad. Talking quietly, both of them looked serious, as though they didn't want anyone else to hear.

As Libby watched, she again felt curious. *I'd give a lot to know what Caleb is saying!*

~ CHAPTER 4 ~

The Bad Start

As the deckhands cast the lines, or ropes, on board, Libby watched from the hurricane deck. With one short blast of the whistle, the *Christina* slid into the current.

Far overhead, black smoke billowed from the tall stacks. From the great wheels on both sides of the boat came the slap of paddles against water.

Libby welcomed those sounds. They brought her back to long-ago days when she and her mother stayed on board. As a little girl, Libby had always felt safe and happy whenever she heard the paddlewheels go around.

Now she breathed deep. To Libby the beautiful March day seemed a special welcome aboard. Then she felt something slap against her skirt. Samson stood there, wagging his tail.

Libby's happiness vanished. "Samson, Samson. I don't know what I'm going to do with you!"

Samson's large brown eyes seemed warm and friendly. But Libby didn't want to be friends.

Trying to ignore the dog, she started across the deck. With every step Libby took, Samson trailed close behind. At the short stairway to the texas deck, Libby picked up her pace. So did Samson.

Outside the door of her stateroom, Libby stopped. "So I've got a pest on my hands!"

As though laughing at her, Samson stuck out his long tongue.

"You have to stay outside," Libby told him.

With a small woof Samson dropped down on his haunches. When he tipped his head, he seemed ready to talk. But Libby shut the door between them.

Inside her room she found her trunk set in front of the door on the opposite side. The trunk made the room even smaller. Yet to Libby's great relief, someone had left water in the pitcher on the washstand. She could clean up.

As Libby pulled off her dress, she found another of Samson's gifts—black hair all over the full skirt.

Libby groaned. *Samson, you are going to wreck my life!*

When Libby tried to put on a different dress, she discovered a bigger problem—the long row of buttons down the back. Never before had Libby needed to fasten them by herself. The harder she tried, the more awkward her fingers felt. At this rate she'd miss the noon meal.

Libby was still struggling with the buttons when she heard a knock on the door.

"Libby?" a soft voice called out.

"Who is it?"

"Rachel Whitney. Caleb's granny. It's time to eat. Can I help you with anything?"

Libby flung open the door. Outside stood a woman much shorter than she. Her gray-white hair was pulled back and twisted into a knot at the top of her head. Smile wrinkles surrounded eyes that made Granny seem young.

"My dress—" Libby said, and the woman went to work on the long row of buttons. "Who did you say you are?" Libby asked.

"The head pastry cook. When I needed work, your father gave both Caleb and me a job."

"Is Caleb all the family you have?" Libby wanted to find out everything she could about this strange boy.

But Granny only said, "I couldn't ask for a finer grandson."

There it was again. Everyone seemed to think so much of Caleb. *Will people ever feel that way about me? Maybe someday I'll have a big never-give-up family that believes in me!*

Granny held a clean dress over Libby's head. "If you hurry you'll still make the officers' table."

As Libby flew down the stairs, she remembered her mother sitting next to her father. Whenever possible, she and Ma had gone with Pa on trips. Even as a young child, Libby had sat at the officers' table with her parents. Strangely enough, the meals had never seemed long.

Pa had often teased her mother. And Ma's laugh—Libby could hear it still. It was like a silvery bell, light and beautiful. Did Pa tease Ma just to hear her laugh?

Now that memory hurt. Libby wished she could laugh with both parents again.

By the time she reached the large cabin that stretched from one end of the boat to the other, Libby was out of breath.

The officers' table was at the front of the cabin, near the boat's office. The captain sat looking toward the tables filled with passengers. Captain Norstad's officers sat with him, according to rank.

"Sorry I'm late," Libby said as she slipped into the chair

on the captain's right. *Thanks to Granny, at least I have a clean dress,* she thought.

Her father had saved the place of honor for Libby. Beyond her sat the pilot, then Mr. Bates, the first mate she had already met. He still seemed resentful that she was there.

On the opposite side of the table sat Mr. Osborne, the chief engineer, and beyond him, the ship's clerk. Libby liked Osborne, the engineer, at once.

"Glad to have you aboard," he said and seemed to mean it. "We hope you'll be happy with us."

Soon the talk swirled around without Libby. She ate quickly, trying to catch up to the others. Yet she felt uncomfortable, even at her father's table. Whenever she glanced toward the first mate, she felt she'd been left outside in a December wind.

Is he upset because I took his room? Libby wondered. *Or is it where I'm sitting?* Because of her, Mr. Bates was one seat farther away from the captain.

Whatever was wrong, Libby knew she had already made an enemy. Only when they were served dessert did Mr. Bates seem to thaw. Libby kept track of the pieces of mince pie he took. Three in all!

When the meal was over, Captain Norstad stopped Libby as she started for the door. "We'll have classes this afternoon."

"You mean *school*?" Libby asked. "I thought I'd get out of that!"

Her father only smiled. "Come to my cabin. We'll start right away."

At one side of Captain Norstad's room on the texas deck was a bed. The rest of the cabin served as a sitting room and place to bring guests. The table that had been filled with maps was now empty except for a book, writing paper, and pens.

Caleb was already there, and Libby chose the chair across from him.

"Do we have to have school every day?" She was starting to feel it might be easier to live with her aunt.

Caleb shook his head. "Captain Norstad can't always teach us. When we're in port, he sometimes has too much to do."

"Good!" Libby exclaimed. "So on those days we get out of school?"

"We still study, but your father doesn't have as much time to teach."

Libby groaned.

"Your father makes school fun."

"*Fun?* What an odd person you are, to think learning can be *fun*!"

Caleb refused to back down. "When we come to a city, your father tells me its history or something important that happened there. Sometimes he asks me to go into town and write up a report."

"About what?"

"Whatever I see happening. He wants me to understand what's going on."

Just then Captain Norstad entered the room. "Well, Libby," he said as he opened a drawer filled with papers. "It will be good having you in class."

As he sat down, he laid three of the papers on the table in front of him. Yet when he started teaching, he never looked at the papers again.

"There's more than one fugitive slave law," Captain Norstad said. "But there's one you especially need to know about—the Compromise of 1850. The law threatens huge penalties for anyone who helps fugitives escape."

"What are fugitives?" Libby asked.

"Runaway slaves," Caleb told her. "Slaves who escape from their owners."

"The law also gives slave owners the right to form a posse and hunt down slaves, even in states that are free," Captain Norstad went on.

"Northern states, you mean?" Libby asked.

Her father nodded. "People in the North don't like the law. Some of the states have passed personal liberty laws that give runaway slaves a jury trial. Other states have told their officials not to help with the capture and return of fugitives."

For Libby this was all new information. *Why don't I know about this?* she wondered. *Is it because Auntie puts away any newspaper Uncle Alex brings home? Doesn't she want me to understand what's going on?*

It made Libby curious. Maybe Caleb was right. This might be interesting, after all. "You said there's a penalty for helping a runaway slave. What kind of penalty?"

"Big fines," her father answered. "Being thrown in jail."

"But isn't that only right?" Libby asked. "If someone breaks a law, shouldn't they be punished?"

Caleb stared at Libby. "Are you serious? Do you understand what this slave law really means?"

"I think so." Inside, Libby didn't feel so sure, but she wasn't going to let on to Caleb.

"You *think* so?" Caleb leaned forward. "If that law is so great, why don't the northern states like it? How come they've passed more laws—ones that give people their personal liberty? Why do the northern states help people to *not* return slaves to their owners?"

"But why don't people return slaves to their owners?" Libby asked. "Most slaves are treated well. They're better off with their masters."

Caleb groaned. "I never in my life thought I'd hear someone say something so stupid."

Captain Norstad spoke more quietly. "Libby, I'm curious. Where did you learn that people are better off being slaves?"

Before Libby could answer, she heard a knock.

"Need your help with a passenger, sir," a man told the captain.

Halfway to the door, Captain Norstad stopped. "Next time we meet, I want to talk more about this. Caleb, you be ready to tell your side of the issue. Libby, you take yours. Be able to give good reasons for what you believe—not just arguments you haven't thought through."

When her father was gone, Libby told Caleb, "I will gladly debate you. And I will win!"

"We'll see," Caleb answered as though she were a pesky fly.

Standing up, Libby gathered together the papers describing the fugitive slave law. All she wanted was to put distance between herself and this hateful boy.

Near the door she stopped. If she weren't so grown-up, she would stick out her tongue at Caleb. Instead she said, "You'll be sorry. You'll find out what a real debate is."

Caleb just grinned. That upset Libby even more. As she hurried out, she slammed the door behind her.

Suddenly Libby stumbled over something. With a whimper Samson scrambled out of her way.

"Oh, Samson!" Libby wailed. She felt bad about stepping

on his paw. "I'm sorry!"

As the door behind Libby opened, Caleb stuck out his head. "You don't even take care of your own dog!"

That's true, Libby wanted to say. *I've never had a dog before.* But she felt afraid to ask for help. Without a backward look, she stepped around Samson and marched away.

"Why don't you let him into your room?" Caleb called after her. "He wants to be with you."

Libby whirled around. "There's no space for him! If Pa wanted Samson with me, he could have gotten a smaller dog!"

"You're exactly the kind of girl Asa Turner wouldn't want brought to the frontier!"

"Asa Turner?" Libby asked. "Who's he?"

"A pastor who lives in the town of Denmark, Iowa."

"So?" Libby asked. She was tired of Caleb trying to get the better of her.

"A while back he asked some young men in Massachusetts to think about coming to Iowa. He wanted them to start churches."

"And they did?"

Caleb's voice softened, but Libby knew he was still upset with her. "Yup. The men who came are called the Iowa Band. Before they started out, Asa Turner told them, 'Get wives who will weave, and spin, and milk a cow, and churn butter, and—'"

"I'm not a wife!" Libby's anger exploded. "And I'm not planning to be a wife for a good long time, *if ever.*"

"Good!" Caleb sounded happy once more, but he wasn't finished yet. "Father Turner said to bring women who are proud of a jean dress or a checked apron."

Libby's hand slipped down between the folds of her skirt.

Feeling the soft, silky cloth, she felt glad that she wasn't wearing either a jean dress or a checked apron. But was Caleb trying to tell her something important—something about herself?

In the next moment Libby found out.

"I still say you're not the kind of girl to live in this wilderness. Even your hair—"

"What's the matter with my hair?"

"How many hours does it take you to make those long curls?" Caleb sounded curious now.

Not for anything would Libby tell him. Nor would she tell him that she didn't know how long she could manage to wear her hair that way. In Chicago she had heated her curling iron by putting it down the glass chimney of a lamp. On the *Christina* she wasn't allowed to have a lamp in her stateroom. The danger of fire was too great.

Reaching up, Libby pulled one of her long red curls. As it sprang back against her cheek, she felt determined to look fashionable, even along the Mississippi River.

"You don't want to tell me?" Caleb's grin spread across his face. "I can find out from Gran."

"Well, go right ahead!" With a toss of her head, Libby opened her door and stepped inside her room. As she started to slam the door, she remembered.

Caleb thinks I'm the kind of girl who can't live in the wilderness. I'll show him! Just in time she held back and closed the door quietly.

Safely inside her stateroom, Libby flopped down on her bed. In that moment she wanted only two things—to be by herself, and to be one thousand miles from Caleb Whitney.

As Libby listened, his footsteps moved across the deck,

then down the few steps to the hurricane deck. When she was sure Caleb was gone, Libby opened the door and picked up Samson's water bowl. From the pitcher in her room Libby poured out water.

Samson's large paws stretched forward and back as he lay on the deck. Directly in front of his nose, Libby set down the bowl.

Leaning forward, Samson swished his great muzzle in the bowl. As water sprayed in every direction, Libby jumped away. But when Samson began to drink, she knelt down beside him to watch.

When the dog finished drinking, he turned his head, as if looking Libby over. As Libby turned back into her room, Samson flopped down across the doorway, as if he had decided to stay.

Inside the room, Libby opened her trunk. Down at the very bottom lay an envelope filled with paper. Next to it was a cherished pencil her uncle had brought home from a business trip to New York.

Sitting down close to a window, Libby started to draw. This was something she did well, and Auntie Vi had given Libby lessons from a well-known artist.

At first Libby's sketch just seemed like long black hair. Then a head started to take shape, and a body. Finally Libby felt satisfied. It was Samson, all right. He even had patches of white hair on his chest and the tips of his toes.

As Libby sat back, she heard footsteps cross the deck. Then someone set something down. Moments later, Libby heard the unmistakable sound of Samson slurping his food.

Libby tiptoed to the door. When she quietly opened it, a

startled Caleb looked up. "I was afraid Samson was hungry," he said.

By the look on his face, Libby knew Caleb expected her to be angry. Instead, she had a question. When she asked it, her voice was soft and humble. "Caleb, will you teach me how to take care of my dog?"

But even as Libby asked, she made herself a promise. *I'll show Caleb I'm not as helpless as he thinks!*

∼ CHAPTER 5 ∼

A Day with Caleb

As the *Christina* steamed toward Saint Louis, Libby remembered her promise to herself. Somehow she would prove to Caleb that she was not a useless society girl.

I'll start by finding jean cloth, Libby decided. *If Caleb sees me in that kind of dress, he'll know I can take care of myself!*

As they came in sight of the city, Libby stood at the railing on the hurricane deck. Along the riverfront, whistles blew and bells clanged. Black smoke billowed up from the tall stacks. Everywhere Libby looked there seemed to be a steamboat easing into the levee, the sloped landing paved with cobblestones.

When the deckhands threw out the lines, she hurried down to the gangplank. Already passengers crowded forward, ready to leave the *Christina.*

"I want to go ashore," Libby said to her father. "I need to buy a few things."

"You can go ashore," he told her. "But I'm not able to go with you. I'll ask Caleb to take you around."

"Oh, Pa!" Libby wailed. Not for all the world did she want Caleb to know what she was planning.

"In some of the towns where we stop you can go alone," her father answered. "But not in Saint Louis. It's a big city, and

I don't want you getting lost."

"I can take care of myself," Libby said quickly.

Captain Norstad shook his head. "I don't know if your aunt let you run around Chicago . . ."

She didn't let me, Libby thought. *I just did.* Not even to herself would Libby admit how often she had come close to big trouble.

Her father's eyes had that serious look again. "Libby, remember how you said you'd like a never-give-up family? A family like that takes care of one another."

Libby looked down. *Even when I want my own way?* She hadn't known that something like this would be part of the package.

"Okay," she said finally. Once more, she met her father's gaze. "I'll go with Caleb." *But I don't have to like it,* she told herself.

When Caleb started toward the gangplank, Captain Norstad called him. As Caleb hurried over, his face looked bright with expectation. Dressed in blue cotton pants and an open jacket, he no longer seemed like a cabin boy. Libby felt sure that he, too, felt excited about going ashore.

But then Captain Norstad said, "Libby would like to do some shopping. I want you to take her."

Suddenly the light went out of Caleb's face. "Does she need to leave right now?" Clearly Caleb did not like this assignment.

"Right now," Libby answered quickly before Captain Norstad could.

Stalking past both Caleb and her father, she started down the gangplank. *How can my own father embarrass me so? Being taken care of by a boy I cannot stand!*

When Libby reached the cobblestone levee, she glanced back. Caleb was right behind her, and her father stood watching them.

"Bye, Pa!" Libby called with a quick wave. But when she turned to Caleb, the smile died on her lips. As she tossed her head, her long curls bounced around her shoulders.

Horse-drawn wagons were everywhere on the levee. Like busy ants, men scurried back and forth, loading or unloading the boats. Some of the men carried large wooden crates on their shoulders. Others rolled barrels toward a gangplank. Between all the freight walked the passengers, making their way to or from the waiting boats.

"I want to go by myself!" Libby told Caleb.

"Believe me," he answered, "I don't like this any more than you do. I thought I'd have one day without you tagging along!"

Libby glanced back. They were out of her father's hearing. "Why don't you just show me where the stores are? I'll find my own way back."

But Caleb shook his head. "I can't let you do that!"

"You can't? Who do you think you are? You're not my boss!"

Caleb sighed. "I'm afraid I am. I wish I weren't."

"You can leave me at the first store," Libby said.

"No, I really can't," Caleb answered.

"Yes, you can." Libby used her most bossy voice. "I'm telling you to."

"I'll lose my job if I leave you," Caleb told her.

Libby stared at him. That put things in a different light. From what Granny said, she and Caleb needed work. Much as Libby despised the boy, she couldn't be that unfair.

Libby sighed. "I guess that means we're stuck with each other."

"For better or for worse." A lopsided smile crossed Caleb's face.

"Mostly worse!" Having Caleb make a joke of it upset Libby even more. "I wanted to walk from store to store, to take my time looking at everything."

"I'm not going to spend all day shopping for girl things," Caleb warned her. "Wherever I take you, you better hurry!"

He set off, walking so fast across the cobblestones that Libby could barely keep up. Only when she crashed into a man carrying a barrel did Caleb stop.

"What do you plan to buy?" he asked when they went on again.

Libby didn't want to tell him. "Just take me to a good store," she said. "I'll find the rest."

Ahead of them lay rows of four- and five-story brick stores. Even Libby felt impressed by their appearance. But Caleb led her beyond them to a store that outfitted pioneers for traveling west. To Libby's great relief, Caleb stayed outside while she went in.

Near the front, large open barrels were filled with apples. Along the wall were bins of sugar and flour. Another section held rakes, shovels, and large picks. Nearby were boots and shoes for the entire family.

In no time at all, Libby found the jean cloth she wanted, as well as thread, needles, and scissors. When she went back outside, her purchases were wrapped in brown paper so that Caleb couldn't see them.

Libby found him leaning against the front wall of the store.

A short distance away, two men talked with each other. Caleb stood with his back to the men, yet something about Caleb's attitude made Libby curious.

As still as a statue, she stayed next to the door. Caleb was listening, all right. But why?

Suddenly he looked up and saw her. Without making a sound, Caleb moved his lips, as though to say, "Shhhhh!"

Her curiosity growing by the minute, Libby waited. Though the sun warmed her face, the wind felt colder than the day before. Even in her warmest coat, she shivered.

From where she stood, Libby couldn't hear even one sentence. But Caleb was just enough closer. He seemed to drink in every word.

One of the men wore a suit Libby knew was the latest style. He even carried a fashionable walking cane. By contrast, the other man wore tattered clothes.

No wonder Caleb was curious. So was Libby. Both men were turned slightly away from her, so she couldn't see their faces. But what she saw, Libby memorized. When she got back to the *Christina*, she'd draw—

In that moment the man with the cane pulled money from his pocket. Quickly he handed it over to the other man. A moment later they separated.

"What was that all about?" Libby asked Caleb when the two men were far enough away.

As though Caleb knew no more than she did, he shrugged. But Libby felt sure he had heard something—something that interested him.

When he refused to explain, Libby became even more curious. *I'll draw their pictures,* she told herself again. *When I get back to the* Christina, *I'll draw both men so I don't forget them.*

Then she remembered. She was almost out of drawing paper, and she needed more pencils.

"Just a minute," Libby told Caleb as she hurried back into the store.

When she came out a second time, she had the large pieces of paper she wanted, along with smaller sheets she could slip into a pocket. She had also found pens and ink, and to her delight, pencils made in New York.

Reaching out, Caleb offered to carry her drawing supplies. "Careful," Libby warned. "There's a bottle of ink."

"Are you done shopping?" he asked, sounding hopeful. "I'll take you to the *Christina.*"

"Do I have to go back?" Libby asked. Even in faraway Chicago, she had heard about Saint Louis. Always she had wanted to see it—the streets, the people, the covered wagons passing through to settle in the new territories.

"Yes, you have to go back," Caleb said, and Libby knew she wasn't going to change his mind.

"I'll just look around," she said. "I'll stay on the streets near the levee—"

"Nope."

"I know my way back." Again Libby felt embarrassed—torn between her desire to see the city and the knowledge that Caleb didn't want her along. "I'll get there by myself."

"Not on your life," Caleb told her. He started toward the river.

Like a fire kindled within her, Libby's disappointment flared up. "I don't have to do what you say! I'm not your slave!"

As Libby spoke, a man walked past them. Dressed in a

three-piece suit and a tall hat, he held only a coat over his arm. Next to him hurried a young black boy, taking two steps to the man's one. Though half the size of the man, the boy carried a bag and two suitcases.

"You don't know what being a slave is all about," Caleb answered quietly. He tipped his head toward the young black with the suitcase.

"That's what I was talking about." Libby thought back to their talk on the boat. "See how that man takes care of the boy? How well dressed he is? He's better off with his master."

"You think so?" Caleb's voice was dangerously low, but sparks filled his eyes. "How come you don't know what's going on? You think that being treated well makes up for being owned?"

"Owned?" Libby didn't feel quite so sure of herself.

"Bought. Sold." Caleb spit out the words. "Like a horse or cow. Like any other property."

Libby pulled back, afraid of Caleb's anger.

He grabbed her hand. "You may come from a mansion in Chicago, but I'm tired of your silly ideas. I'm going to show you something."

"Like what?" Libby asked. "You better take care of me, or Pa won't like it."

"I'll take care of you, all right!" Caleb pulled her along. "I'll take you to something you should have seen a long time ago!"

CHAPTER 6

Strange Message

With quick angry steps Caleb headed away from the river. Libby hurried behind, trying to keep up. But Caleb's long strides kept her running.

In the street around them, teams of horses pulled heavily laden wagons. Caleb darted between them, seeming not to notice the danger. When they reached a building with tall pillars, he finally stopped.

"Where are we?" Libby asked.

"The courthouse for Saint Louis County," Caleb answered, his voice short with anger.

Wide steps led up to great wooden doors. As more and more people moved into the area, Libby's gaze was drawn toward the top of the steps.

A man stood there wearing a long, expensive coat that protected him against the sharp wind. Looking out over the people, he seemed to swagger, as though taking pleasure in the size of the crowd.

In front of the steps was another white man who stood like a guard over a tall, strong-looking black boy. The boy waited with head bowed, as though staring at the ground.

Libby turned toward Caleb. "What have you brought me to?"

Caleb's gaze met hers. "A slave auction."

"A slave auction? Pa won't like that one bit."

"Are you going to tell him?" Caleb asked, and she knew he was daring her.

Seconds later, Caleb looked away, as though he'd forgotten Libby. Instead, he seemed to watch the tall black boy.

Even from this distance, Libby could tell that his short-sleeved shirt and cotton pants were new. *It's just like I said. Well cared for, that's what he is.*

Wanting to continue their argument, Libby faced Caleb. "See his clothes?"

Her words made Caleb even more angry. "They cleaned him up to sell him!" he muttered close to her ear. "Gave him new clothes to bring a better price!"

Again Caleb grabbed her hand. When he pulled Libby through the crowd, she had no choice but to follow. Finally Caleb could not get around any more of the men waiting for the auction. Yet from where Caleb stopped Libby heard the guard talking to the young slave.

"They call you Jordan, boy? You're too uppity for my taste! Don't you forget for one minute who you are! You is *property*!"

The guard pushed the boy forward. "Hear me now? Keep your eyes on your feet, or they'll think you run every chance you get!"

As Jordan started up the steps, he moved slowly, as if dreading what lay ahead. Libby stood on her tiptoes. Inside she felt torn—wanting to see, yet not wanting to see.

In spite of his strong appearance, Jordan seemed to have trouble walking. One at a time, he swung his feet wide with an awkward movement. Partway up the stairs, he stumbled.

The man in the long coat called down to him. "Hurry, boy! Get up here!"

Moments later, Jordan reached the top of the steps. Only then did Libby see that his feet were bare, even on this cold day. She also saw why he swung his feet wide and stumbled.

Around his right ankle was a heavy steel band. Another band circled his left ankle. Between the leg-irons stretched a chain.

Libby gasped. Caleb turned to her, a warning in his eyes. Quickly Libby covered her mouth, trying to hide her dismay. Yet when she looked back, the chain was still there. The leg-irons were still in place. She could not wish them away.

As the man on the steps raised his arm, the crowd grew quiet. Libby no longer needed to be told what was happening. The well-dressed man was the auctioneer.

"We got a boy here you'll all want to own," he started out.

The young slave stood straight and tall with shoulders back. Yet his face looked blank. His head bowed, he stared down at the steps.

With every onlooker turned his way, the auctioneer seemed to enjoy the attention he was getting. "Turn around, boy!" he commanded.

Boy? Libby asked herself. *Or young man?* She had thought Jordan was fifteen or sixteen—a bit older than Caleb. Now she wasn't sure.

As Jordan turned, the chain on his leg-irons clanked. When he faced the front again, he stared out beyond the crowd, as though he did not see the people.

Watching him, Libby felt strangely moved. *He's like royalty.* The thought surprised her. How could a young black seem like a king?

Suddenly a lump filled Libby's throat. She looked away, not wanting to see someone only a few years older than her being sold.

Caleb's low, angry voice reached her ear. "You better watch. You better know what you're talking about."

"Real property this one is!" The auctioneer's voice called a warning, as if reminding the slave of his place.

Instantly the young man bowed his head. Once again he stared at the steps.

"Able to do a man's work, I tell you. Give this boy the hardest labor you got, and he'll do it."

The crowd laughed.

"This here boy will do a man's work and work a man's day. But you won't have to feed him as much as a man. Show 'em your muscle, boy!"

Reaching out, the auctioneer pinched Jordan's arm. "Hear me now? Show 'em your strength!"

As though disliking the command, the young black lifted his arm slowly. When he flexed his muscle, the crowd roared its approval. Yet Jordan's face held no expression.

"Good healthy slave too." With one quick movement the auctioneer stuck his finger in the boy's mouth. Running the finger around inside Jordan's lips, he asked, "See his teeth?"

Jordan swallowed hard. For one second his resentful eyes flicked toward the auctioneer. Then Jordan's face again went blank.

Sudden nausea swept through Libby. Just watching the auctioneer, she gagged, wanting to vomit.

"What am I bid for this fine piece of property?" he sang out.

Libby gasped, filled with the awfulness of it.

But Caleb spoke in her ear. "Hush!"

Instead, a great river of grief washed over Libby. Tears welled up, blurring her vision. Turning away, she bowed her head, unable to watch.

This time Caleb touched her arm in warning. "Don't make a scene!" His whisper sounded kinder now.

Libby closed her eyes, unable to watch. But she could not shut out the sound of the bidding.

"Five hundred!"

"Six hundred!"

From close by, a man called out, "Eight hundred!"

Surprised by the two-hundred-dollar raise, Libby opened her eyes. The man in front of her led the bidding. His back was turned toward her, but somehow he seemed familiar.

"One thousand!" called another man, and a murmur passed through the crowd.

A white-haired gentleman had given that bid. Suddenly Libby hoped that Jordan would go to him. *Maybe he'd be kinder,* Libby told herself, then wondered where the thought came from.

"Twelve hundred!" shouted the man in front of Libby.

Gold covered the handle on his cane, and Libby felt sure it wasn't used for walking. Short in height and slender around the waist, the man wore a suit of finely woven, expensive-looking cloth. Yet there was something about his back—

"Oh no!" Caleb muttered, as though he'd heard Libby's thoughts. "Old man Riggs!" Even the name seemed to fill Caleb with dread.

"Who's Riggs?" Libby asked.

"A slave trader. He makes big money buying slaves and selling them to other people."

As Caleb spoke, the man turned enough to show Libby the side of his face. In that moment she knew who he was—the man she had watched in front of the store.

For one instant he glanced around. As Libby looked into his cold blue eyes, she had no doubt that Riggs was the cruelest man she had ever seen.

"Thirteen hundred!" the white-haired gentleman called out.

"One thousand, five hundred!" Riggs answered.

A ripple of sound passed through the crowd. Everyone knew that fifteen hundred dollars was a lot of money.

"Top dollar for someone Jordan's age," Caleb whispered.

The auctioneer looked toward the white-haired gentleman, who shook his head, and withdrew from the bidding.

"Fifteen hundred once." The auctioneer paused. "Fifteen hundred twice." Again he paused. "Sold for one thousand, five hundred dollars!"

Again a murmur moved through the crowd. Jordan had become an unusual piece of property.

As the slave started down the steps, Caleb again pushed forward. But Libby stood like stone, still upset by all she had seen.

"Hurry up!" Caleb prodded, and she came to life.

Moving quickly, Caleb worked his way around the rest of the onlookers. When he reached the courthouse steps, he slowed down. Then Caleb looked as if he had nothing important to do.

The change in Caleb made Libby curious. What was this

strange boy planning? Whatever it was, Caleb wouldn't explain. She'd have to find out for herself.

When Jordan and his guard reached the bottom of the steps, Caleb was close by.

Jordan's new owner, Riggs, was even closer. "Over here, boy!" Even his voice sounded mean.

As the slave and his owner stood next to each other, Libby felt a jolt of surprise. Jordan was more than a head taller.

If he was aware of the difference in height, Jordan did not show it. Nor did he forget himself long enough to glance up. Instead, he stared at his bare feet.

Riggs looked Jordan up and down, then growled a warning. "No slave ever got away from me! Alive, that is!"

In Jordan's cheek a muscle twitched. No other sign showed that he had heard the trader's threat.

For a minute longer Riggs looked him over. Then, as if satisfied that Jordan understood, the trader turned away. Leaving Jordan under the care of the guard, Riggs walked over to pay for his new slave.

With his gaze on the trader's back, Caleb edged closer to Jordan. Libby followed. By the time Caleb stood next to the young black, Libby was right behind, where she could watch both of them.

Strangely, Caleb still looked as carefree as if he were out for a Sunday stroll. Hands in the pockets of his jacket, he seemed to be watching the people pass up and down the courthouse steps. But the moment someone spoke to Jordan's guard, Caleb leaned close to Jordan.

"Alton," he whispered in Jordan's ear. "Tomorrow night. The *Christina*."

As though no words had passed between them, Jordan did not look at Caleb. Only a slight nod of his head told Libby that he had heard.

Again Caleb edged forward. This time he stopped just ahead and to one side of Jordan. In the dirt Caleb's foot moved quickly, spelling out letters—C–H–R–I–S. . . .

In that instant Riggs turned around. When he started back to Jordan, Caleb did not look down. Instead, he shuffled his feet just enough to wipe out the letters.

By the time Riggs reached Jordan, Caleb had slipped into the crowd. Libby followed close behind. Not until they were a block from the courthouse did Caleb slow down enough for her to speak.

"What was that all about?" she asked.

But Caleb only told her, "If you ever need to know, you'll find out."

~ CHAPTER 7 ~

The Judas Goat

All the way back to the river, Libby tried to figure Caleb out. One moment she thought he'd be someone nice to know. The next moment she couldn't stand him. Yet whatever her thoughts about Caleb, they didn't seem to matter to him. Libby felt sure he'd be pleased if he never saw her again.

When they reached the *Christina*, two sturdy boards had been set next to the usual one to widen the gangplank into a ramp. Along the sides of the ramp were fencelike boards, placed as guardrails.

There's more than one gangplank? Thinking back, Libby remembered the bloodhounds sniffing at the gangplank in Burlington. The dogs had turned away as if finding no scent. Had Caleb put out a different gangplank?

On the levee near the *Christina*, several goats wandered around, seeming confused. When two men chased them, the goats hid behind barrels and boxes.

Directly in front of the ramp stood a large male goat. A tall, heavyset man stood next to the billy, trying to get the goat on board.

Wanting to stay out of the way, Libby stood aside and waited. As she watched, the man tugged the rope around the goat's neck. The billy refused to go up the ramp.

"If he could just get the Judas goat in, he'd be okay," Caleb said.

"The Judas goat?" Libby asked. "What do you mean?"

"That male goat is the leader. Wherever he goes, the rest will follow—even if it's to a slaughterhouse."

Seeming to use every one of his muscles, the man shoved, pushed, and prodded at the Judas. As though ready for battle, the billy planted his four hooves and refused to budge.

Finally the man moved around to the goat's head. Grabbing hold of a long curved horn, he tugged. When Judas tossed his head from side to side, he swung the man as well.

With a disgusted shake of his head, the man gave up. Turning around, he called up the ramp to a deckhand. "Hey! Come here! Help me!"

Just then Judas lowered his head and butted the man's back end. As the man fell flat, Judas bounded around him and up the ramp. Libby tore after the goat with Caleb right behind.

"Grab him!" Libby shouted to the first deckhand she saw. As the man headed for the goat, Judas leaped to the top of a fenced-in area. When the deckhand grabbed for him, Judas danced along the rail, then jumped down. Across the deck he darted, turning this way and that. One man tried to tackle him. Another landed just behind his sharp hooves.

Reaching the stairway, Judas leaped upward, taking three or four steps at a time. As though finding a mountaintop, he stopped on the second deck. Just then, a waiter carrying a large tray rounded the corner.

Judas lowered his head. From a dead stop he ran straight for the man. A hair's breath away from the waiter, the billy

darted aside, clipping the man's knee.

For one moment the tray wobbled. As the waiter fell, food splattered across his white jacket. Dishes crashed to the floor. Broken china flew in every direction.

Trying to keep her footing, Libby circled around the shattered china. Through the open door into the cabin Judas fled with Libby and Caleb after him. By now the other goats followed as well. Behind them raced three or four men, each trying to catch a goat.

Judas headed for the nearest white tablecloth. As he plowed under the table, the cloth caught on his horns. Glasses and china landed with a crash.

Under the table, Judas pawed the floor, then came out on the other side. The next goat caught the cloth on his back, but Libby scrambled after Judas.

Toward the opposite end of the cabin Judas rushed. More than once, Libby got close. Each time, the billy changed direction and darted out of reach.

When he circled yet another table, Libby saw her chance. With a great leap, she landed on the goat's back. Grabbing his horns, Libby hung on. But Judas kept running, taking her with him.

"Libby!" Caleb shouted. "Let go!"

Libby refused. Halfway down the cabin, the goat headed for a long velvet curtain. Straight toward the wall he ran. At the last minute he turned just enough to knock Libby off his back.

As she landed on the floor, she heard a loud rip. The curtain tumbled around her.

Fighting her way out, she saw Judas headed once more toward the far end of the cabin.

Oh no! Libby thought. Desperately she scrambled to her feet. With Caleb close behind, she again tumbled after Judas.

When he upset another table, Libby almost caught him. This time Judas ran straight toward the floor-to-ceiling mirror at the end of the cabin. In front of the glass he slid to a stop. Staring into the mirror, he saw his reflection.

Judas stamped his foot. The goat in the mirror stamped his.

Again Judas stamped his foot. "No one's coming into my territory!" he seemed to say. Again the goat in the mirror stamped back.

Filled with panic, Libby raced after Judas. The goat lowered his head.

"Libby!" Caleb cried, but she did not stop.

As Libby reached out for the horns, something dropped over her head. In the next moment she heard a mighty thud, then the crash of shattering glass. Like a statue Libby froze, knowing she must not move.

When Libby pulled the cloth from her head, she saw it was Caleb's jacket. Seeming dazed by what had happened, Judas stood in front of the wall, shaking his head. Splinters of glass lay on his back and the surrounding floor.

Turning around, Libby saw Caleb just behind her. "You stopped me!" she sputtered. "I could have caught him!"

"Could you now?" Caleb asked.

His question struck Libby funny. The large deckhand trying to load the goat had not been able to handle Judas. Why did she think she could manage?

Looking down the long cabin, Libby saw the mess. Tables overturned. Dishes across the floor. Velvet drapes ripped from their rods. Suddenly Libby doubled over with laughter.

Caleb joined in. "It *is* funny!" he said, when he could talk again.

As their gaze met, all the anger that had been between them disappeared. For the first time Libby saw Caleb as he really was—a boy almost the same age as she, a boy who might be fun to know.

Then Libby looked down. In one hand she still held Caleb's jacket. For the first time she saw the splinters of glass caught in the cloth.

With her other hand she reached up to her face. Carefully she felt her cheeks, her chin, her forehead, her eyes. It frightened her, just thinking what could have happened. But she found no cuts.

"You knew, didn't you?" Libby's voice was soft with wonder.

"Yup," Caleb answered. "I knew."

"I might have been scarred for life. How could you think so fast?"

Caleb shrugged, as though what he had done wasn't really that special. Then he grinned. "Just keep it in mind when you think you can get the best of me!"

Suddenly Libby felt overwhelmed by all that had happened. Unable to answer Caleb, she wanted only to flee.

When Libby reached the texas deck, Samson stood up from where he lay next to the door of her stateroom. His unexpected welcome warmed her.

Libby glanced around. No one was there to see.

Feeling unsure about what to do, Libby stretched out her hand. When she patted Samson's head, he stood quietly, as though liking Libby's uncertain touch.

Again she looked around. This time she stroked Samson's back. As Caleb said, the dog's coat was shiny and clean. Wherever Libby stroked the wavy hair, it fell back into place.

When she turned away, something had changed. Deep down, Libby felt glad that Samson was there.

Inside her stateroom, she shut the door. Yet she could not shut out all that had happened—the Judas goat and her own narrow escape with the mirror, but so much more.

There, where no one could see, Libby started to tremble. As if she were freezing cold, her entire body shook. Caleb had wanted to shock her by taking her to an auction. He had certainly succeeded!

As though they were pictures Libby had drawn, images marched across her mind. The auctioneer, selling off a human being. The evil-looking man who had bought Jordan. And then Jordan himself.

As much as she wanted to forget him, Libby couldn't. Each time she thought of Jordan, one idea returned: *royalty*. But royalty had to do with kings, men who ruled a nation. How could someone who was a slave remind her of a king?

Taking out her paper, pen, and ink, Libby started to draw. She had planned to sketch the slave trader. Instead, she drew Jordan's straight shoulders, his proud head, and the dark eyes that forgot and looked for one moment beyond the crowd.

After all the uncertainties of the day, Libby found comfort in seeing a picture take shape. When she finished, she knew why Jordan reminded her of royalty. It was more than the way he stood. Though a slave, Jordan had a purpose in life.

That surprised Libby. *How can I believe something like that about a person I've never met? It's my imagination!*

But the idea would not leave her. She tried to think about other people who had a purpose in life. One of them was Pa. Even when she was little, Libby had known that he wanted to do business in a way that fit with his beliefs about God.

"I could take shortcuts," Libby heard him say, "but it wouldn't be right."

"You can only do what is honest," Ma answered. "That's the way you are. You live according to what you believe."

Pa nodded. "If I didn't, I couldn't live with myself."

"We'll make it through the winter anyway," Libby's mother told him. "We always do."

In her younger years Libby hadn't understood what her parents meant. Yet their words had gone deep into her mind, so deep that she had never forgotten.

Now she tried to remember if there was a winter of hardship, a time of suffering because her father hadn't earned enough. Libby couldn't recall such a time. She only remembered how much her mother and father loved her.

Yes, Pa had a purpose in life. Libby didn't always understand or agree with that purpose. But Pa knew how he wanted to live and where he wanted to go.

Standing up, Libby looked out the window. How could Jordan be the same way, especially when he had no choice about where he wanted to go and what he wanted to do? In a slave owner's eyes, Jordan was *property*!

All her life Libby had wanted to have her own way. To pick her friends and what they would do together. Jordan couldn't even do that.

Never before had Libby seen one tiny peek into the life of a slave. Until today she had not felt one small emotion about what a slave child would feel. But now the picture of Jordan standing on the courthouse steps would not leave her.

As Libby studied her drawing, she began to weep. From the deepest part of her being came great sobs. With her face buried in her pillow, Libby cried until she could cry no more. Much as she wanted to forget, she could not push Jordan's suffering aside.

When Libby finally cried herself out, she went to the pitcher and poured water into the basin. The cold water would not hide the red splotches on her face. Nor could that water wash away the redness of her eyes. Yet Libby Norstad knew she would never again be the same person.

Her hands were still shaking as she laid out the jean cloth on the floor. To Libby's surprise it felt good to be back with one thing she did know. Auntie had taught her to sew.

When her hands grew steady, Libby took up the scissors and cut out a skirt. As she worked, she felt impatient with the lace-covered dress she wore. Even the stiff crinolines that made her skirts spread wide seemed a waste.

Going to her trunk, Libby lifted the cover. From inside, she lifted out one expensive dress after another. For one brief moment she touched each of them, feeling the soft cloth and enjoying the colors. Her best times with Auntie Vi had come while they were shopping. *Is that why I like my dresses so much?*

Close to the bottom of the trunk was a pale green dress that reminded Libby of her mother. Both Auntie Vi and Uncle Alex had told Libby how beautiful she looked in that dress. As though carrying her favorite doll, Libby had taken that memory into a school party. There her friends told her the same thing.

I'll save it, Libby thought as she smoothed the cloth. *Even if I wear jean cloth, I'll keep this dress for when I want to look my very best.*

At the bottom of the trunk Libby found the dress she wanted to wear—a simple cotton dress—a calico with three colors. When she slipped it over her head, Libby felt better.

Yet when she looked into the mirror, she giggled. Her long tight curls didn't match the dress. *It's as though I can't decide who I am!*

Libby took up her hairbrush. With swift movements she brushed out her long curls. At first her long hair just went back the way it was. But finally Libby's deep red hair hung loosely about her shoulders.

Picking up the front strands, Libby tied them with a ribbon at the top of her head. The rest of her hair fell down her back, long and wavy, curling only at the ends.

When Libby left her room, she felt like a different person. By taking her to a slave auction, Caleb had forced her to think in a new way.

Going down the stairs for supper, she met Caleb coming up. In the midst of the stairway he stopped. Libby caught his glance toward her hair, then his look of approval.

A quick grin lit his face. "You're not a society girl anymore."

That was all he said, but Libby knew Caleb liked the change. She had to admit that she did too. Though it would take getting used to, she almost felt like herself, not someone Auntie Vi wanted her to be.

"Caleb," Libby said quickly. "You said you'd help me with Samson. Can you figure out what he knows?"

"How smart he is?" Caleb asked, and Libby knew he was ready to tease. For the second time that day Caleb seemed like a boy who could become a friend.

"What commands Samson knows," she answered. "What I should do to get him to obey."

"That shouldn't be hard," Caleb told her. "I'll meet you on the hurricane deck after supper."

Even as Libby agreed, her thoughts leaped ahead. *And I'll find out what you're trying to hide, Caleb Whitney!*

CHAPTER 8

The Underground Railroad

When Libby went into the cabin for supper, the broken glass had been cleaned up. Tables and chairs were upright, and the velvet drapes once more in place. A large bare piece of wood showed where the mirror had been.

Libby knew that the extra work had put the *Christina* behind schedule. *Will we still reach Alton tomorrow night?* she wondered. *If we don't, will it make a difference to Jordan?*

As soon as supper was over, Libby found Caleb on the hurricane deck.

"I know a lot of the usual commands for dogs," he told her.

Because of the way Samson jumped up the first day, Libby often thought of him as a puppy. Other times he acted like a grown dog. To her great relief, she had already discovered he was housebroken. What else did he know?

"Here, Samson," Caleb said, and the dog looked up at him with great wags of his tail.

When Caleb said, "Sit," Samson sat. When Caleb said, "Stay," the dog stayed in one place, even though Caleb walked away.

"Good dog!" Caleb praised each time Samson did something right. Caleb also discovered that Samson would stay alongside Libby if she took him for a walk.

"I wonder what else he knows," Caleb said. "If we had a little wagon . . ." His voice trailed off as he thought about it. "We do have a wagon! A small one for carrying groceries from the gangplank to the galleys. If I fix it up a bit . . ."

Caleb led Samson and Libby down to the main deck. When he found the wagon, Caleb used strong rope to make a padded harness. When everything was ready, he showed Libby what to do.

The harness went in front of Samson's chest, over the top of his back, and behind his front legs. Caleb attached two long poles to the front of the cart and connected them to the harness. Then he attached a leash to Samson's collar.

Through it all, the dog stood still, waiting patiently until everything was ready.

"He might be used to this," Caleb said finally. "Now let's see what he knows."

Kneeling down in front of the dog, he motioned Samson forward with his hands. "Come," he said, over and over.

At first Samson didn't seem to understand. Caleb repeated the command.

"Come," he said, still eye level with the dog. Suddenly the dog took one step toward him.

"Yay!" Caleb praised him. "Good dog, good dog!"

Once again he commanded, "Come." This time Samson obeyed at once. Again Caleb praised him.

Standing up, Caleb took the leash. As he held it above the dog, Caleb walked forward. As though Samson had followed all his life, he padded after Caleb. Now and then Caleb gave a slight jerk on the leash to remind the dog where he should go.

Each time Samson obeyed.

Caleb gave Libby a turn with Samson, then unhitched the wagon. "His owner must have spent a lot of time training him," Caleb said. "Samson wouldn't know this much otherwise."

"Aren't you going to try more?" Libby asked.

Caleb shook his head. "I want to stop while he's still having fun. Then he'll want to do it again."

Just then Libby remembered that she had planned to find out what Caleb was up to. As she sat down on a large box on one side of the boat, she asked, "What do you think happened to that young slave we saw yesterday?"

"Jordan?" Still petting the dog, Caleb sat on a small barrel. "The man who bought him is a slave trader. Of all the people I know, Riggs has the worst reputation."

"For being cruel?" That wasn't hard for Libby to understand.

"He doesn't just beat his slaves because they've done something wrong. He beats them to make sure they *don't* do something wrong."

Libby had never heard of such a strange way of thinking. "So no matter how hard a slave tries to do everything right, he can't please Riggs?"

Caleb's blue eyes reflected his worry. "It's as though Riggs has to prove he's boss."

"Aren't there any slave owners who are kind?" Libby asked.

"Sure," Caleb answered. "Some owners treat their slaves like family. And the house servants really are. A Negro mother brings up the master's children. Sometimes those children feel really close to their mammy."

"Because the mammy takes care of them all the time?" Libby understood that too.

"But is it *kind* to keep someone a slave?" Caleb asked. "And a lot of owners don't care what happens to Negro families. They sell husbands away from wives, children away from parents."

Libby felt like weeping again. She knew what it meant to be separated from a mother by death, from a father by distance. "If a slave runs away, the owner hires a slave catcher." Caleb leaned forward, wanting Libby to understand. "The owner offers a big reward if the fugitive is caught."

Now he'll tell me! Libby felt sure she could find out whatever she wanted to know.

"Caleb," she asked, "what did you mean when you whispered to Jordan?"

Suddenly Caleb grew quiet. "You heard me whisper?"

Libby nodded. "You said, 'Alton. Tomorrow night. The *Christina.*'"

"You're sure that's what you heard?" As though it weren't important, Caleb leaned back against the railing.

"I'm sure," Libby answered. "And why did you bring out a different gangplank in Burlington?"

"In Burlington?" Caleb sounded like an echo.

"When the three Negro men came aboard."

Still Caleb's expression did not change. "Different gangplank," he said, as if still thinking. "What do you mean by that, Libby?"

"The *Christina* has three planks. When they're put together side by side they make a ramp."

"Oh yeah. That was the ramp Judas went up." Suddenly Caleb laughed. "In all the time I've been on this boat, I've never seen anything as funny as those goats running through the cabin."

Libby laughed along with him. "It was funny, wasn't it?" She remembered how she flung herself after the goat, how she had tumbled off when he brushed her against the wall. Now it seemed ridiculous.

Caleb's grin lit his face. "Next time we have a goat run loose, I'm going to send you after him!"

As they kept talking, the sun set over the city of Saint Louis. The rose-colored sky felt like the warmth in Libby's heart. Again Caleb seemed as if he could be a friend.

Yet, alone in her room that night, Libby realized something. *I still don't know what Caleb is doing!*

~

The next morning Libby saw men carry a large mirror on board. "I'm glad we're in Saint Louis where I could find such a mirror," Pa told her.

While the ship carpenter set the mirror in place, the deckhands finished loading the *Christina*. As a packet boat, she carried both passengers and freight. In addition to the goats that were now penned up, there were barrels filled with sugar, salt, and molasses. Wooden boxes held pots and pans, saws and shovels, wood stoves, candles, and soap.

Some of these needed supplies had come from the Ohio River on steamboats like the *Christina*. Other freight had come up the Mississippi River from New Orleans.

During the afternoon Libby watched from the hurricane deck as passengers streamed on board. Many of them were immigrants who planned to carve out a life in the wilderness for which the Mississippi River offered a road.

As the water in the boilers heated up, smoke poured from the tall stacks. At last the gangplank was pulled in. While passengers found their places in the cabin or on the deck, the *Christina* steamed up the river.

Between ports Libby and Caleb were supposed to get their schooling. When Libby reached the captain's cabin, Caleb was already there. Once again, they sat at the large table facing each other. Libby wanted to ask him questions, but there was something she had learned: Caleb would not answer unless he wanted to.

When Captain Norstad came through the doorway, Libby felt extra glad to see him. She'd ask him what she wanted to know, and she'd ask in front of Caleb.

At the first opportunity Libby began. "When slaves run away, where do they go?"

"North," her father answered. "They follow the North Star. When they can, they cross over rivers like the Mississippi or the Ohio into free states."

"Like Illinois?" Even as she asked, Libby watched Caleb.

Captain Norstad nodded. "From this area, fugitives often travel across Illinois to Chicago or some place near Chicago. If they reach Lake Michigan, a helpful steamer captain hides them on his boat. He takes fugitives to a place where they can pass into Canada."

"And freedom?" Libby asked. "But how do they get this far?" Libby was still watching Caleb's face.

"Sometimes they figure out a good escape plan and travel a long distance alone. Other times they find a free black or a white person connected to the Underground Railroad."

"A railroad? What do you mean?" Libby was starting to think that she knew the answer.

"Usually it isn't a real railroad, but it can be," her father explained. "The Underground Railroad is a secret plan to help runaway slaves reach freedom. A house that takes in fugitives is called a *station*. The person who lives there is an *agent*. Whoever leads the runaway to the next safe place is called a *conductor*."

Aha! Libby thought. Caleb's face still offered no hint of what he was thinking. Yet for the first time Libby felt she had gotten the better of him. At least she was able to put some pieces together.

But then her father asked, "Are both of you ready to tell me your ideas about the fugitive slave laws?"

"I am, sir," Caleb answered quickly.

Libby squirmed in her chair.

"Libby?" her father asked.

Nervously she pulled forward a long strand of red hair. Until yesterday she would have done anything to beat Caleb Whitney in a war of words. Today she didn't have the heart to try.

"Libby?" the captain asked again.

As Libby twisted the hair around her finger, she decided what to say. "I'm not ready, Pa."

"Do you need more time?"

"Even if you gave me more time, it wouldn't help. I don't want to talk about the law."

"Oh?" Captain Norstad shot a glance toward Caleb, then looked back at Libby. "I think you'd do a good job of telling me your ideas. Why don't you want to try?"

Libby opened her mouth. She wanted to say, "Because I saw a slave auction." But she saw Caleb's look. In Saint Louis he had dared her to tell her father. If she did, Caleb would never trust her again.

Libby's thoughts raced. *How can I explain without telling Pa what happened?*

Finally she drew a deep breath. "I've been doing a lot of thinking." Scared now, as well as nervous, she stumbled over the words. "I've changed my mind about some of the things I said."

Again Captain Norstad glanced toward Caleb, then back to Libby. Before her father's clear eyes Libby's gaze fell. Someday she would tell him what she now believed about slavery. But not now. Not yet.

When Pa didn't ask her to explain, Libby felt relieved. Just the same, there was something she knew. When they reached Alton, Illinois, that afternoon, she'd be on deck. She would watch every move Caleb made.

As though she had just heard his whisper, she remembered the words: "Alton. Tomorrow night. The *Christina*."

~ CHAPTER 9 ~

Caleb's Secret

Late that afternoon Libby and Caleb stood on the hurricane deck of the *Christina*. A few miles above the place where the Missouri River flowed into the Mississippi, Libby caught her first daytime view of Alton, Illinois.

In the rugged hillside on the right bank of the river were large gray buildings with a long wall. "Is that a castle?" Libby asked.

"The Illinois state prison," Caleb told her.

Tall warehouses hugged the shore. Above them, church steeples pointed to the sky. Somehow they offered comfort to Libby, as though here were people who believed in something. The thought surprised her, for often she felt uncertain about her own beliefs.

When the *Christina* nosed into the flat rock that formed a natural wharf, Caleb hurried down to the main deck. To make sure that she saw whatever he did, Libby followed him.

By now, the setting sun cast long shadows across the river into the town. As the shadows lengthened, the crew started unloading freight. In the growing dusk a watchman placed a torch in an iron basket hung out beyond the bow of the boat. As the pine torch flared up, burning coals dropped into the water.

Like other steamboats her size, the *Christina* used about twenty-five cords of wood during every twenty-four hours of travel. That meant stopping at least twice a day to take on more fuel. The process was called *wooding up.*

In the eerie light of the flickering torch, men began carrying wood from great piles along the river. Up and down the gangplank they hurried with three-foot-long logs balanced on their shoulders. Passengers earning the price of their ticket worked along with the crew, stacking the wood near the furnaces or on deck.

As a cold March wind blew across the water, Libby shivered. Pulling her coat around her, she thought about the wood stove in the cabin. Though its welcome warmth drew her, Libby felt unwilling to leave the deck. What was supposed to happen this night?

Now and then she caught a glimpse of Caleb carrying wood along with the men. When nearly every available space was filled with wood, Libby knew they needed even the place where she stood. She started toward the steps.

Ahead of her, a man carried two heavy logs on his shoulder. Realizing that he could see on only one side, Libby stepped out of his way. Just then the man stepped the same direction, crashing into Libby.

As one of the logs tumbled onto the deck, she leaped back. The heavy piece of wood just missed her feet.

Suddenly Caleb was there. "You're in the way," he said. "Why don't you watch from the steps?"

"That's where I'm trying to go!" Shaken by her narrow escape, Libby again started in that direction. Partway there, she turned back to see who the wood carrier was.

Just then Caleb stepped between Libby and the man. "You all right?" Caleb asked.

"I'm all right!" Libby exclaimed. But she had no doubt that she could have been badly hurt.

When she reached the stairs, she again tried to get a glimpse of the man's face. By now his back was toward her and his new-looking pants dragged on the floor. Because his cap was pulled down and the collar of his coat turned up, Libby couldn't see even the hair on his neck.

With one quick movement Caleb picked up the dropped log and added it to the man's load.

"No wonder he couldn't see!" Libby called to Caleb.

Glancing toward Libby, Caleb grinned, then leaned close to talk to the wood carrier. Without turning even slightly, the man nodded.

Inside, Libby felt a nudge. *There's something familiar about him. What is it?*

Leaving the stairs, she hurried forward. Again Caleb moved between her and the wood carrier. Before Libby could reach the man, he walked away.

"C'mon, race you to the cabin!" Caleb said. "Let's get in out of the cold!"

His sudden friendliness surprised Libby. In the large, main cabin Caleb found a place in the circle of people surrounding the wood stove. Nearby, Libby took another opening and stretched out her hands to the warmth. After the cold wind, the heat of the stove felt good.

Soon one of the female passengers spoke to Libby. "Aren't you the captain's daughter?"

"Why yes, I am," Libby answered, feeling pleased.

When she finished talking with the woman, Libby glanced around. *Caleb! Where is he?*

A rush of anger flowed through Libby. It wasn't hard to figure out that Caleb had used his chance to disappear. And Libby wasn't willing to let anyone turn her into a fool!

Then a bigger question entered her mind. *What is Caleb trying to hide?*

~

From one end of the *Christina* to another, Libby searched for Caleb. She felt sure she would find him in the engine room on the main deck. The great steam engines were there, as well as the large furnaces that heated the water to make the engines run. Yet Caleb wasn't there, nor in the blacksmith shop.

Finally Libby made her way to the dessert and pastry kitchen. Located in front of one of the huge boxes that housed a paddlewheel, the galley was spotlessly clean.

Granny was kneading bread, but the warm scent of bread dough didn't fit with the way Libby felt.

"Your grandson is the strangest boy I've ever met!" she blurted out.

"Strangest?" Granny's blue eyes studied Libby. "What do you mean?"

"Caleb just asks questions. He never gives answers!"

"About what?" Granny asked.

"You're just like him!" Libby exclaimed.

"And what does that mean?" Granny gathered up a great mass of dough, turned it around, and folded it over.

"I think I saw a young slave come on board," Libby answered. "But when I asked Caleb about it, he wouldn't tell me. In fact, he sneaked away."

"Without telling you anything?" Granny punched the dough.

"Not a thing!"

For an instant Granny seemed to relax. Then Libby decided she had imagined it.

"So you think Caleb is strange?" Granny asked.

"With any other boy I've met I could ask anything. All I had to do was smile." Libby put on the smile she often practiced in front of a mirror.

"And the boys would tell you," Granny finished.

"Whatever I wanted to know."

"And Caleb doesn't." With the ease of long practice Granny shaped the dough into a large ball and set it in a wooden bowl. For some reason she seemed very satisfied with herself—and with Caleb too.

But then Granny surprised Libby. "Do you know how to make bread?"

Libby shook her head. "In Chicago our cook always did it." At lunch and dinner on the boat, Libby had seen how everyone wolfed down the good bread. Libby liked it, too, but had given only a passing thought as to where it came from.

"I'll show you how," Granny said. "You'll be good at it in no time."

She wrapped a large apron around Libby. Soon Libby had it covered with flour. At Auntie Vi's she would have called this *work* and stayed far from it. Here with Granny it seemed like fun.

More than once, the dough stuck to the board, and Libby's hands felt clumsy and awkward. Finally she started to get the feel for what she should do. By that time she was curious about

Granny and why she and Caleb were here on the *Christina*.

"Caleb's father was my son," Granny said softly. For a moment her busy hands stopped moving. "When he and his wife died, Caleb came to live with me."

"*Both* of his parents died?" Libby asked.

"Within a few days of each other. They died of cholera."

Libby knew about that dreaded disease. Sometimes it wiped out entire families—or left only one or two members of the family to struggle on with life.

"Caleb was only four years old. For a while we stayed where I lived after my husband died. Then I needed to earn more—to set money aside for Caleb growing up. We came here."

For a time Libby was silent, punching her dough until finally Granny said, "That's enough. You don't want to kill it."

Libby laughed, but she was thinking about Caleb. "I still say he's the strangest boy I ever met."

"No," Granny said, and her voice was soft again. "You just have to understand Caleb. You need to understand what he believes in."

"What *does* he believe in?" Libby asked.

Granny only smiled. "I think you need to ask Caleb."

There it was again—something mysterious about the boy. From Granny, Libby learned that he was fourteen, almost fifteen, only one year older than she. Libby also knew how Caleb looked. Blond hair that fell over his forehead, close to his blue eyes. Almost the same height as she was, but stronger and quick.

Beyond that, Libby knew almost nothing. What was it about Caleb that she couldn't understand? Whatever it was, Libby knew she'd get no more information from Granny. In that, too, Granny and Caleb were alike.

"Have you fed your dog tonight?" Granny asked.

Libby shrank back. No, she hadn't. How did Granny know about that?

"I saved some leftovers for him," Granny said as she went to find the bowl. "Tell you what. You come down here every morning and every night. I'll give you what you need."

"Thanks, Granny." Libby scooped up the bowl. Once again she felt embarrassed. Embarrassed that she had forgotten about her own dog. Embarrassed that she had so much to learn.

How can I be so helpless? Libby wondered as she left the galley. But inside, she was changing. *I'll learn,* she thought. *I'll surprise them all!*

On the way up the steps to the hurricane deck, Libby met Caleb. Stopping on the narrow stairway, she cut off his escape.

"You know that man who dropped the wood?"

Caleb nodded.

"I don't think he was a man at all."

"Oh?"

In the eerie light of the pine torch, Libby saw Caleb rest his hand on the railing. His face held no hint of a secret.

"He wasn't a grown man," Libby said. "But he was tall and about your age."

Without speaking, Caleb waited.

Libby hurried on. "He looked like someone I've seen before."

"He did?" Caleb asked.

This time Libby recognized Caleb's game—asking questions, instead of giving answers.

"Why is Jordan on board?" she asked.

On the railing Caleb's hand tightened. No other movement gave away his surprise.

"Why do you think you saw him?" Caleb's voice still sounded calm, as though whatever she answered wasn't very important. "It was dark, you know, and there were a lot of people."

"But Jordan was with them," Libby answered. "I'm sure of it."

She leaned forward, trying to see Caleb's eyes. Not even an eyelash flickered.

"By the way," he asked, "have you walked your dog today?"

Libby flared up. "I'll walk my dog when I want to!"

Caleb grinned. "I thought you asked me to help you."

Libby whirled around. She was all the way up the steps before she realized Caleb had tricked her again.

He's outsmarted me at least three times! How could I let him do that to me?

Libby made up her mind. He wasn't going to fool her even one more time!

Whatever game you're playing, Caleb Whitney, I'm going to find out what it is!

～ CHAPTER 10 ～

Libby's Choice

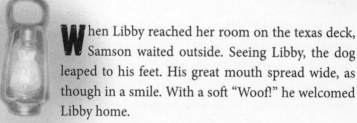

When Libby reached her room on the texas deck, Samson waited outside. Seeing Libby, the dog leaped to his feet. His great mouth spread wide, as though in a smile. With a soft "Woof!" he welcomed Libby home.

Suddenly she felt ashamed. Samson really was a nice dog, and she hadn't even remembered to feed him.

Kneeling down, Libby reached out her hand to stroke the dog, as she put down his dinner. When Samson licked her face, Libby scrambled out of the way. She wasn't quite ready for that!

As though he were starving, Samson gobbled up the food. Again, Libby felt ashamed.

"I'll do better, Samson," she promised. "I'll remember after this."

She also remembered to take him for a walk. With the great black dog at her side, Libby strolled up and down the riverfront next to the *Christina*. Each time she gave a slight tug on the leash, Samson obeyed.

The dark waters of the Mississippi River flowed silently past her father's boat. The torch still flickered, casting an eerie light. For the first time that evening the wharf was quiet, and so was the city of Alton. Even the oil lamp that often burned in the large cabin of the *Christina* offered no light.

"C'mon, Samson," Libby said after a time. "We better go in."

The moon was up now, and its light reached where the flickering torch did not. Just then Libby caught a movement on the texas deck outside Pa's cabin. One shadow—no, two—crept close to the wall. Seeming to glide along, the shadows stepped onto the hurricane deck, then started down the stairway.

The first shadow was halfway to the deck just below when moonlight lit his face. Caleb! Libby knew there was something he was trying to hide. *Something? Or someone?*

When Caleb moved on, the second shadow passed into the moonlight. Jordan! Libby was sure of it! How did he manage to escape from the slave trader who owned him? Had Jordan and Caleb gone to Pa's cabin, but found he had stepped out?

With a warning hand on Samson's head, Libby crouched down next to a pile of freight. In the darkness she strained to see. If she was going to find out what Caleb was doing, she had to know where he went. If the dog barked . . . but Samson didn't.

Soon the two boys reached the main deck. Turning, they crept back under the overhang along the side of the boat. When they disappeared through a doorway, Libby ran for the gangplank. On board, she tied Samson's leash to the railing and raced after the boys. Moments later, she slipped into the engine room.

From somewhere deep in the room came the clank of metal against metal. As Libby crept toward the sound, she heard voices.

Slowly, quietly, Libby crept forward. When she peered

around a boiler, Jordan stood with his bare foot next to a block of wood. One leg-iron circled his ankle. Another lay on the floor.

Only two days before, Libby had seen Jordan's leg-irons up close. The irons looked like handcuffs, but were used around ankles instead. Now the chain between Jordan's feet was broken. Two cloth rags told Libby that he had tied the ends of the chain around each ankle. Somehow, somewhere, Jordan had found a jacket and pants long enough to hide the leg-irons.

"Hold still again." Caleb wedged a padded cloth between the iron circle and Jordan's skin.

Watching them, Libby wondered again how Jordan had managed to escape. How had he reached the Christina with the heavy irons around his ankles?

Using a hammer, Caleb pounded a cold chisel, cutting the rivet that held the leg-iron together. Before long, Jordan's second leg-iron fell away.

"You made it this far!" Excitement filled Caleb's voice. "Tomorrow we'll take you to a safe place up the river."

A wide grin flashed across Jordan's face. As if throwing off all the suffering he had known, he raised his arms in triumph. Standing tall, he stretched as high as he could reach. Again he reminded Libby of royalty.

Tears welled up in Libby's eyes. She wanted to rush forward. She wanted to celebrate Jordan's escape from his cruel owner. Instead she remembered. *I'm not supposed to be seeing this!*

Quickly Libby backed away. She had almost reached safety when she bumped into an oilcan. When it clattered against metal, Libby started to run.

"Stop!" Caleb called after her.

As she kept running, Caleb called again. "I see you, Libby! Stop!"

His voice was low, and Libby knew he didn't want to be heard. Yet Caleb expected her to obey.

When he caught up, he grabbed Libby's arm, and she had to stop. "What did you see?" he asked.

"N–n–n–nothing," Libby stuttered.

"You're lying. What did you see?"

Libby had no choice but to tell him. "I saw you take off Jordan's leg-irons. I saw Jordan stand tall, excited that he's gotten this far. But if he's found, Pa could go to prison for hiding a runaway slave on his boat."

Caleb loosened his grip on Libby's arm. "So you understand, after all."

"I understand," Libby said softly. "I wish I didn't."

"Then you know the cost," Caleb answered. "Will you keep the secret?"

Again Libby thought of her father. "I don't know if I can keep the secret."

"You can't tell *anyone*!" Caleb told her. "If you do, Jordan's life is in danger!"

Libby straightened to her full height. Up till now she had felt awkward about being almost the same height as Caleb. For the first time she felt glad.

"Don't you tell me what to do, Caleb Whitney. I won't listen to you—not ever!"

Libby turned and broke into a run. Near the gangplank she snatched up Samson's leash. By the time they reached the texas deck, Libby was panting. Only then did she realize that Caleb hadn't followed her.

When she opened the door of her room, Samson stayed on the deck, as though unsure what to do. Until now Libby had never allowed him past the threshold. This time Libby urged the dog inside. "Go on. It's all right."

When Samson dropped down next to her bed, he took nearly every inch of the floor. It was just as bad as Libby had expected. But tonight she didn't care. She just wanted the dog beside her.

By the light of the moon, Libby slipped into bed. Lying there, she looked up to a ceiling she couldn't see.

Jordan is safe now! Libby hoped it would be forever. But then she felt uneasy.

Jordan still needed to reach some place far away from slave catchers. Perhaps he could hide in a northern state, but greater safety lay in Canada. That meant he would have to travel all the way across Illinois to reach a steamer captain on Lake Michigan. Hiding during the day, he would move on at night. Whether there was dry land, swamp, lake, or river, Jordan would have to go across, around, or through.

Always someone would follow: a slave catcher greedy for the reward his capture would bring, a man with dogs trained to sniff out Jordan's scent. Like a criminal Jordan would be chased and hunted. Every moment of the day and night he would need to think not only of his own safety but also of the people who helped him.

With all her heart Libby wanted Jordan to reach safety. Each time she tried to fall asleep, Libby remembered the evil face of the slave trader—the cruelest man Caleb knew. If Jordan went back to that owner, he would beat Jordan, possibly to death. Libby dreaded the terrible thought.

Then she remembered the fugitive slave law and her worry about Pa. *Caleb said I can't tell anyone. Does that anyone include my own father?*

In spite of their disagreements, Libby wanted to be friends with Caleb. She wanted him to like and respect her. *If I tell Pa, what will Caleb think?*

The March night felt cold, and there was no heat in Libby's room. She drew the quilts over her head, but the cold in her bones came from something worse than the night air. *I didn't know that being a never-give-up family would cost so much.*

~ CHAPTER 11 ~

Code of Honor

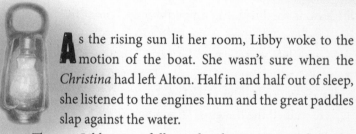

As the rising sun lit her room, Libby woke to the motion of the boat. She wasn't sure when the *Christina* had left Alton. Half in and half out of sleep, she listened to the engines hum and the great paddles slap against the water.

Then, as Libby came fully awake, there was something she knew. *Pa is my father—my family. When I came to live on the* Christina, *we promised to help each other. A never-give-up family sticks together. I owe Pa more than I owe someone who might be a friend.*

The moment she was dressed, Libby searched out her father. She needed to talk to him now, even before breakfast. When she found him in his cabin, they sat down at the large table.

A strand of Pa's hair fell down over his forehead, and he pushed it back. As always, Libby felt proud of him. But there was something more. *After all the years when I hardly saw him, I don't want anything to separate us. Not even my fear of what Caleb thinks.*

Libby started by telling about the large wooden box dropped on the *Christina's* deck. She told how she had watched that box being loaded onto the train at Gulfport.

Giving her every bit of his attention, her father listened. "Go on, Libby," he said. "What else do you want to tell me?"

Libby skipped over the slave auction and went straight to the night before. "I saw a runaway slave, Pa—a fugitive. I saw Caleb take off his leg-irons."

"You're sure that's what they were?"

Libby reached for a piece of paper and a pen. Glad for the art lessons she'd had, she dipped the steel point into ink and quickly drew a picture.

Captain Norstad leaned forward. "Those are leg-irons, all right. It's hard to remember that only a few days ago you didn't know about the fugitive slave law."

He studied the drawing. "Can you tell me how you found out what leg-irons are?"

Libby felt the warm flush of embarrassment creep into her face. That part of the story—seeing Jordan at an auction—she hadn't planned to tell. If she did, would Caleb lose his job?

As she wondered what to say, someone knocked on the door. Libby felt relieved.

"Come in," her father called.

Caleb stood there. Seeing him, Libby's relief vanished.

"Do you want to talk to me?" the captain asked as Caleb drew close to the table.

"In a minute, sir." Caleb looked from one to another. Then his glance dropped to the table. In full sight lay Libby's drawing.

Quickly Libby laid her hand across the picture. But it was too late. Looking up, she saw Caleb staring at her, his eyes bright with anger.

"What is it, Caleb?" The captain leaned back in his chair, as if he hadn't noticed a thing.

But Libby knew better. Her father's brown eyes took in everything. In her entire life Libby had never fooled him once.

"Could I speak with you alone, sir?" Caleb asked.

"What would you like to talk about?" the captain answered.

"I'd rather not say, sir." Caleb's gaze flicked over to Libby, then back to the captain.

"It's all right, Caleb," Captain Norstad said.

The boy shook his head. "I'll wait, sir."

"It truly is all right." As if wanting to be sure Caleb understood, the captain sounded strong and confident.

But Caleb's eyes were filled with doubt. Never before had Libby seen him hesitate before making up his mind.

In the silence a clock ticked. Libby's thoughts raced ahead. *Caleb knows so much. Is he what they call a railroad conductor?*

Finally Caleb spoke. "I don't trust Libby, sir."

"But I do," the captain answered.

For a moment longer, Caleb waited. "We've taken on a valuable book with black covers," he said, as though speaking against his will. "The label is blurred, and I don't know where to send it."

"Be so good as to bring the book here," Captain Norstad answered.

"Now?" Caleb looked shocked.

"Right after breakfast. Be very careful about the book's safety."

For the first time since Libby met him, Caleb could not hide his feelings. As if hoping the captain would change his mind, the boy backed out of the room.

Even that bothered Libby. She realized that no one else took as much freedom as Caleb when talking to her father.

Like a green-eyed caterpillar, envy wormed its way into Libby's mind. She envied Caleb's relationship with her father.

As though understanding her thoughts, Captain Norstad turned back to Libby. "There's something we need to talk about—what it means to trust one another. Do you trust me?"

Libby sighed. "I want to. It's the reason I came to talk with you, but—" She stopped, afraid to go on.

"But what?"

"Caleb doesn't trust me."

"That's something else," her father answered.

"Is it?" Suddenly Libby felt angry. Angry about all the things she didn't understand. All the things that made her afraid. Angry, even, at the bond between her father and Caleb.

Before she could hold back her words, they tumbled out. "Why do you like Caleb more than me?"

"I don't like Caleb more than you." Pa's voice was quiet but firm. "I love you both—each in your own way."

As though thinking about how to explain, the captain stood up and walked around the room. Finally he stopped next to Libby's chair. When she refused to look at him, he reached down and cupped her chin in his hand. Gently he lifted it.

"Look at me, Libby." He waited until she turned her gaze to his.

"I love you as a daughter, Libby. You are priceless to me. I also love you as a person—a very special person."

Like a dam before a great river of water, something inside Libby broke into pieces. In those endless months between visits she had built a wall between herself and her father. As long as she could remember, Libby had wanted his love.

Still she held back, dancing away from that wounded place

deep within. "But Caleb? You seem to—" Libby struggled to find the words. "You seem to trust him."

The captain nodded. "I do. I would trust Caleb even with my life."

"Your *life*?"

"Yes, I would. I think I'd better explain."

Sitting down at the table, her father faced Libby again. "When Caleb came on board, I started him out with easy jobs, things he could do as a cabin boy. Soon—"

"You found out how much he can do," Libby said. In these few days she had often felt surprised by how grown-up Caleb seemed. At times she found it hard to believe he was fourteen, almost fifteen, only a year older than she.

"Caleb knows how to handle responsibility," Captain Norstad explained. "We believe in the same things."

Libby leaned forward. Maybe she could find out what was really going on.

"Caleb and I share the same code of honor," Pa explained. "We both want to live for things we believe in."

"But what does that mean?" Libby didn't feel satisfied.

"To start with, Caleb and I want to protect runaway slaves. When Congress passed that fugitive slave law in 1850, it was a bad law. Many Christians believe the law goes against the way God intends for us to live."

"I don't understand," Libby said.

"God tells us, `Love one another, as I have loved you.' He wants all of us to be a never-give-up family, Libby. He created us to be equal. Does that sound like anything you know?"

Of course! Libby had memorized the words. "'We hold these truths to be self-evident, that all men are created equal . . .'"

Now the meaning of those words came alive. "The Declaration of Independence!"

"Yes! That all of us are created equal," Pa said. "That we are endowed by our Creator with 'certain unalienable Rights, that among these are Life, Liberty, and the Pursuit of Happiness.'"

"Unalienable?" Libby asked. "I never did know what that means."

"Not to be taken away. Rights that shouldn't be taken away," Pa explained.

The night before, Libby had seen Jordan reach an important step in his search for freedom. *But I didn't even know what the word* freedom *means!*

It came as a shock to her. "If that's what our country believes, why do we allow slavery?"

Pa smiled but did not speak.

In that moment Libby realized something. "It's not just our country. It's *me*. A few days ago, I said such stupid things. How could I forget the Declaration of Independence? How could I act as though the words aren't important?"

Trying to sort out her thoughts, Libby jumped up and walked over to a window. Far below, the river ran cold and dark with the fullness of spring. Watching it, Libby remembered: *There's more. Something I still don't understand. Pa doesn't know everything that's going on. Not even on his own boat.*

Libby turned back to her father. "I'm scared, Pa," she said. "I want Jordan to be free, but I'm scared that you'll go to prison."

"There's always a risk when you believe in something," her father answered. "You took a risk in talking to me, didn't you?"

Libby nodded.

"I may have to pay the cost of what I believe."

"This code of honor you and Caleb have—"

A knock sounded on the door. When it opened, Caleb poked his head into the room. "Breakfast, sir."

As Libby and her father hurried down the steps to the decks below, she caught a quick glimpse of the shore past which the *Christina* steamed. When they entered the large main cabin, everyone else was already seated. Up till now, Libby had loved eating Granny's good breakfast rolls. For the first time Libby could hardly swallow them. She only wanted breakfast to be over.

The minute she finished eating, she asked to be excused. Standing up, she started away from the table.

Just then a loud crash shook the boat. Above the pop of snapping timbers, a woman screamed. As the boat shuddered, Libby lost her balance.

Suddenly she fell to the floor. Even the boards trembled beneath her hands.

~ CHAPTER 12 ~

Let My People Go!

Near Libby, a dish slid off the table. Again the woman screamed. Then a child cried out.

Filled with terror, Libby pushed her arms against the floor. *Why am I here? What happened?*

When she tried to sit up, panic washed over her. *Is the boat going down? What should I do?*

Then, through the haze of fear, Libby saw her father. He stood near his table, asking for attention. Captain Norstad looked amazingly calm.

As Libby scrambled to her feet, she found that the floor was in its right place. It also seemed perfectly level. The sound of engines had stopped, but the boat didn't lean to one side.

"Be quiet, please," the captain called out in his strong voice. "There's no need to panic."

As the first mate hurried into the room, an uneasy silence fell over the passengers. For a moment Captain Norstad listened to Mr. Bates.

When the officer left again, Captain Norstad told the passengers, "You'll be glad to know that the damage isn't serious. One of the paddlewheels caught a floating log. The damage will slow us down, but it's not dangerous. We'll have you in Burlington soon."

One by one, the passengers sat down. Soon the buzz of conversation filled the cabin again.

Still feeling shaky, Libby followed her father out to the deck. When they reached the broken paddlewheel, the damage looked even greater than Libby expected. Part of the housing, the arched wooden box that surrounded the wheel, was splintered beyond repair.

Because of the break, Libby could see down into the paddlewheel. Shattered arms and wooden cross-pieces lay every which way.

"How come there's so much damage?" Libby asked as Caleb came to stand beside her. For the moment she had forgotten the anger between them.

"When the log got caught, the wheel must have thrown it around," Caleb told her.

The damage looked so bad that Libby couldn't understand how they would keep going.

Caleb explained that too. "We have two engines. Each engine runs a different wheel. We'll make it to Burlington with the engine and paddlewheel on the other side."

Caleb no longer looked angry, but now he dropped his voice. "Don't forget what I said last night."

"About Jordan?" Libby spoke in a whisper, but even so, Caleb shushed her.

"It's his life, you know. Don't tell anyone besides your father. Not even one other person."

A thousand questions leaped to Libby's lips. *It's okay that I told Pa? Then why can't I tell anyone else?* As Libby left to check on Samson, she wondered about it.

When she found that the dog was all right, Libby went to

her father's cabin. Though she knew he had to make plans for the broken paddlewheel, she felt impatient about every moment of delay. Soon after she heard an engine start, the captain entered his cabin.

Caleb was not far behind. "Do you still want to see the black book?"

When Captain Norstad nodded, Caleb hurried out. Soon he returned.

"This is Jordan Parker," Caleb said as he brought the tall young man into the room.

Jordan's new-looking pants dragged on the floor, almost covering his bare feet. *Do those long pants hide wounds left by the leg-irons?* Libby wondered.

"Jordan wants to stay on the *Christina*," Caleb went on.

"You know it's dangerous," the captain told Jordan.

The young man nodded. "Yes, sir." As though he were still on the courthouse steps, he stood straight and tall. Yet he kept his gaze on the floor.

"If we let you off in Quincy or some other place in Illinois, you could cross the state on the Underground Railroad. At Lake Michigan a steamer captain would take you to a place where you could pass into Canada. You would have your freedom."

Suddenly all of Libby's scared thoughts came rushing back. *If Jordan is found—*The danger frightened her. Yet Pa and Caleb and Jordan—none of them acted as if something unusual was going on.

"Why do you want to stay on the boat?" the captain asked Jordan.

"Before Christmas, sir, Old Massa sell my daddy. Momma

and me—we ain't got no idea where he is. But we wants to run away before Old Massa sell the rest of us. Before he take my sisters and my brother and pull them from my momma's arms."

Libby flinched.

"While I tries to find a way for us to run, Old Massa sell Momma and my sisters and my brother. Sells them up north from where I is. While I still thinkin' how to collect them and run, Old Massa dies."

"So you were sold in Saint Louis?" Captain Norstad asked.

"Yes, sir."

"Jordan escaped from his new master," Caleb explained. "The slave trader Riggs."

"Riggs?" A grieved, angry look crossed the captain's face. "You got away from Riggs?"

"Yes, sir. And now I wants to go back, sir."

"To a man like Riggs?" Captain Norstad sounded puzzled.

Jordan shook his head, but he still looked at the floor. "No, sir. I wants to find my momma and my sisters and my brother to bring them out. Momma can't do it by herself. I needs to bring them cross the river."

"To the Promised Land?" Libby's father seemed to know the answer.

But Libby wondered about it. The Mississippi River flowed between the slave state of Missouri and the free state of Illinois. Was that what Pa meant?

Then she remembered. Long ago, Ma had taught her about Moses taking the Israelites out of slavery in Egypt. Forty years later, Joshua led them across the Jordan River into Canaan, the Promised Land.

A smile broke across Jordan's face. "Yes, sir. When I was

born, Momma call me Jordan. I was jist a little boy when she say, 'Jordan, you is goin' to take our people cross the river. You is goin' to lead our people to the Promised Land.'

"'What you mean, Momma?' I ask her. Before long, I didn't need to ask no more. I believed what my momma tell me would be true."

As though Libby still saw Jordan on the courthouse steps, she remembered. Somehow she had sensed that he knew what he wanted to do with his life. *Purpose*, she called it. *Jordan has a sense of purpose.*

Captain Norstad leaned forward. "How were you and your mother going to reach the Promised Land?"

"We was goin' to follow the North Star, sir. We was goin' to find the men with the broad-brim hats. Momma say, 'If we gits there, we be safe. Those men with broad-brim hats, they show us how we git to the Promised Land.'"

"And now?" the captain asked. "What's your plan?"

"Caleb say we is goin' near the people with the broad-brim hats."

"The Quakers at Salem, Iowa?" Captain Norstad asked.

Caleb nodded.

"I wants to go there, sir. I wants to know if Momma got my family out."

"But what if they aren't in Salem?" The captain's dark eyes looked worried. "There'll be slave catchers looking for you. They'll know that if they haven't found you in Missouri, you'll be in Iowa or Illinois. There must be a huge reward on your head."

Still looking at the floor, Jordan shrugged.

"There's a big risk that you'll be taken back into slavery," the captain warned. "If you leave the boat, I can't protect you."

For the first time Jordan forgot himself and looked up. "It's a risk I gots to take, sir. How can I be free when my family ain't?"

When the room fell silent, Captain Norstad stood up and paced around the table. From long experience, Libby knew that he was thinking.

Finally he stopped in front of Jordan. "I need another cabin boy like Caleb. Would you like the job?"

Astonishment spread across Jordan's face. "Yes, sir! Then I can stay?"

"You can stay. If anyone asks what you're doing here, tell them you're my cabin boy. For every day you work, I'll give you a day's wages."

"You *pay* me, sir?" Jordan looked as though he couldn't believe such an offer. "You foolin' me, sir?"

Captain Norstad shook his head. "But there's something you have to promise me."

"Yes, sir."

"Whenever we come into port, you go down and help Mr. Osborne. He's the man who works where Caleb took off your leg-irons."

The engine room, Libby thought. *Where Jordan is out of sight from people on shore.*

The quick flash of understanding in Jordan's eyes told Libby that he knew exactly what the captain was saying.

~

When Caleb and Jordan left the room, Libby stayed at the table. There was a thought she couldn't push aside. *Caleb knows Pa better than I do!*

Again Libby felt a twinge of jealousy. She wasn't sure what to do about it. She only wanted to make up for all the time she and her father had lost.

"Pa?" Libby asked. There was something she needed to say, but she didn't know where to begin. "You know what you told me before?"

So much had happened between then and now, but Captain Norstad understood. "That I love you."

"I love you, too, Pa," Libby said.

When her father opened his arms, she walked into his big hug. Libby felt glad that he had given her the words to say.

~

Often the *Christina* logged ten miles an hour going upriver. Now, with the use of only one paddlewheel, she seemed to limp along. Yet the rudder held her straight against the current.

Later that afternoon, as Libby rounded the texas, she came up behind Caleb and Jordan. Away from passengers and most of the crew, Jordan had his shirt off. On the sunny side of the deck, he sat with his back turned to the warm spring sun.

As Libby watched, Caleb dipped a cloth into a bowl of clean water. When Libby started to back away, he called to her. "It's all right," he said quickly. "You can come."

In a few more steps Libby saw what Caleb was doing. Gently he washed the great open wounds that crisscrossed Jordan's back.

Libby gasped. *Whip marks!*

Turning, Jordan looked up in her face. "I don't want no pity."

"You don't have my pity," Libby answered quickly. "You

have my respect." *And my sadness,* she added to herself.

"Riggs beat him," Caleb explained.

Libby didn't have to be told. The red lines crossed Jordan's back, as if the whip had been laid one way, then another. *Is that what happened in just one night of being owned by Riggs?*

Feeling as though she could barely breathe, Libby remembered what she had said about slavery. *How could I be so stupid?* Though Jordan didn't know what she had said, Libby wanted to tell him she was sorry. But she couldn't get out the words.

"Don't you hate Riggs?" she asked instead.

She wanted to close her eyes, to run away from the sight of Jordan's back. Yet somehow Libby knew Caleb was testing her about something she didn't understand. If she was going to pass that test, she had to stay.

Just the same, Libby walked around in front of Jordan where she couldn't see his back. "Don't you hate Riggs?" she asked again.

"I wants to be angry." Jordan didn't look at her.

His words reminded Libby of the one small flash of resentment she had seen at the auction.

"I wants to hate him with all my soul—" Jordan went on, "But if I hate him—"

Even sitting on the deck, Jordan looked tall. He held his hand about three feet above the boards. "When I was jist so high, my daddy say to me, 'Jordan, you is goin' to git lots of hurts in life. No matter what happens to you, don't you hate.'"

"Don't hate?" Libby blurted out. How could Jordan help but hate someone who had whipped him this way?

"'Jordan,' my daddy say, 'hatin' robs your bones of strength, makes you blind when you needs to fight. If you forgive, you be strong.'"

"Forgive? When someone treats you like that?" Without warning, tears welled up in Libby's eyes.

She tried to speak, to say that she was sorry for what had happened to Jordan. Again, she couldn't find the words.

But Caleb tried. "I don't know if I could forgive that way."

Turning, Jordan looked up at him. "You could, Massa Caleb. If you ain't got no choice, you could."

"But how?" Even to her own ears, Libby's voice sounded faint with the impossibility of it.

"I tells myself I is goin' to forgive," Jordan answered. "With every lash of the whip I whisper to myself, 'I forgives you, white man.' Then I remember what my momma say long ago. 'No one else is goin' to suffer like this. Jordan, you is goin' to take your people out of Egypt.'"

Egypt. Where the people of Israel had suffered in slavery, even as Jordan had. When Libby looked up, she saw that Caleb was still watching her. She wondered if she had passed whatever test he was trying to give.

Then she no longer cared about Caleb. She only hurt for Jordan. From deep within she felt a great sorrow about what had happened to his people.

But Jordan seemed to have forgotten both her and Caleb. As if reaching back into a world of his own, he closed his eyes and started humming. Then he began to sing, quietly and softly, as if afraid of being heard. Libby leaned forward to catch the words.

"*When Israel was in Egypt land—*"

Jordan's lips moved in a whisper. "*Let my people go!*"

"Oppressed so hard they could not stand—" Swaying back and forth, Jordan seemed to forget himself.

"Let my people go!" Like a cry it came—a cry from deep within.

> "Go down, Moses,
> Way down in Egypt land—
> Tell ole Pharaoh
> Let my people go!"

In spite of the lashes laid across his back—or perhaps because of them—Jordan sang on. When at last he opened his eyes, Libby saw the glad light of hope.

∼ CHAPTER 13 ∼

Riggs!

It's too dangerous for you to go there," Caleb told Jordan as the *Christina* steamed toward Burlington.

The two boys and Libby were sitting on the texas deck again, talking about the Quaker community of Salem. In southeastern Iowa, Salem was not far from the slave state of Missouri.

"If Momma found the people with the broad-brim hats, I kin find her," Jordan answered without looking at Caleb.

"I'll hunt up your mother for you," Caleb promised. "Gran and I lived in Burlington for a while. I'll ask questions there first. Then I'll go to Salem."

But Jordan shook his head no. "If you find Momma, she won't know if she kin trust you. She'll be feared to come."

"Riggs could have taken a faster boat," Caleb warned him. "He might already be in Burlington, looking for you."

The risk seemed to make no difference to Jordan. "I gots to find Momma myself."

Caleb sighed. "You know what the fugitive slave law says. A slave owner can form a posse anywhere—even in a free state like Iowa. Riggs can hunt you down wherever you are."

A posse? Was that what I saw my first night in Burlington? Libby wondered.

"I knows the danger, Massa Caleb."

"Master Caleb?" Caleb leaned forward as though trying to get Jordan to look at him. "I don't feel right about having you call me that. Will you just call me Caleb?"

Silence fell between them as Jordan seemed to think about it. "It be mighty hard," he said finally. "But I kin try."

"Good!" Caleb exclaimed. "Now you said you know the danger."

"Yes, sir." Jordan stopped. For the first time his gaze met Caleb's. "Yes, Caleb. I knows the danger, but the Lord, He is my protection."

With that Caleb no longer argued. "Then we've got three days. Captain Norstad says it'll take that long to fix the paddle-wheel. We need to be back by the third night so he can make up for lost time."

Three days, Libby thought. Right now it seemed forever. What could three days mean to Jordan? What if he found his mother and his sisters and his brother? But for Pa, wanting the early spring trade on the river, three days was a long time.

When the *Christina* limped into Burlington, immigrants on board rushed to the railing. Like a mighty wave, they poured down the gangplank. For them, Burlington was the door to the new state of Iowa and territories beyond. Here they would make a home and begin a new life. Yet for Jordan, stepping off into Burlington might mean just the opposite—the loss of his hard-won freedom.

From her stateroom Libby watched Caleb and Jordan mingle with the immigrants on the landing. As they started up the street, they walked apart from each other. Yet Caleb turned more than once, as though keeping an eye on Jordan.

Seeing them, Libby made up her mind. Quickly she put paper and a pencil in a pocket of her skirt. At the door on one side of her room, she peered through the window. Samson lay on the deck just beyond.

Without making a sound, Libby opened the door on the opposite side, slipped through, and closed it behind her. Carrying her shoes, she crept down the short ladder, making only a slight thud on the deck below. But when she tiptoed toward the next stairs, she heard the soft pad of paws crossing the deck behind her.

Libby whirled around. "Samson! What are you doing here?"

His mouth spread wide, Samson seemed to laugh at her. His tail wagged, as if saying, "We're friends, aren't we?"

Libby groaned. "Okay, you can come. But only as far as the gangplank."

Samson lowered his head, as if promising to obey. When Libby reached the gangplank, she turned around. "Sit!"

Samson dropped down on his haunches. His tail wagged, thumping against the deck.

"Good dog!" Libby petted Samson's head. "Good boy!" When Libby's arm came within range, Samson licked it.

"I know your tricks!" Libby exclaimed. As Samson started to wiggle, she commanded, "Stay!"

As though grieved with the command, the dog tipped his head.

"Stay!" Libby told him again. This time she backed away. The dog obeyed.

When Libby reached the landing, she turned and looked back. Samson still sat on the deck. With sad dark eyes, he watched Libby leave him behind.

Once on shore, Libby soon caught sight of Caleb and Jordan. They still walked apart from each other, with Jordan slightly behind Caleb. Libby stayed just far enough behind so that neither boy saw her.

From the riverfront, the streets of Burlington rose upward in bluffs and hills. Several ravines—narrow valleys between the hills—divided the land. Through some of those ravines dirt roads brought farmers with their horses and wagons into town. Deep ruts showed where oxen had pulled covered wagons and pioneers westward.

Around Libby, the streets seemed alive with excitement. Men, women, and children hurried in or out of stores. Now and then Caleb stopped at one of them to ask questions. Always Jordan waited outside, mingling with whatever people were around. When Caleb moved on, Jordan followed a short distance apart.

Tall and straight, he walked as though sure of where he was going. More than once, heads turned as people watched him. It didn't bother Libby until she spied a piece of paper lying on the ground. She snatched it up.

$200.00 Reward.

Runaway from the subscriber,

a black boy named

JORDAN PARKER,

about 15 or 16 years of age, about six feet tall, last seen wearing tattered cotton shirt and faded blue pants. It is presumed he will make for Iowa or Illinois. I will give one hundred dollars if taken in the State of Missouri, or above reward if taken outside that State and held for me . . .

As Libby glanced at the bottom of the notice, the name Riggs leaped up at her. Without reading the rest, she stuffed the paper in her pocket. Even if an abolitionist pulled down this notice, how many more were around? How many people had seen this description of Jordan? How many of them wanted the great amount of money he would bring?

Filled with panic, Libby started walking as fast as she could without calling attention to herself. Jordan and Caleb needed to be warned.

They were less than a block apart when Libby came up behind a man who looked familiar. A tall hat hid his face and hair. Short and wiry, he moved as if he would act quickly on anything he set out to do.

Each time Caleb and Jordan stopped, the man also stopped. Whenever they walked on, he stayed just the right distance behind. Because Libby had done the same thing herself, she couldn't help but notice.

With growing uneasiness, she edged closer. The man wore an expensive suit and carried a cane with a gold handle.

Seeing it, Libby's stomach tightened with dread. The next time the man stopped, she edged forward enough to see his face. As though doing cartwheels, her stomach turned over.

The slave trader, Riggs! Jordan's owner!

Then Riggs moved on. *What's he waiting for?* Libby wondered in panic. *Does he want more men to help him capture Jordan?*

When Riggs stopped to look into a store window, Libby hurried around him. Walking fast, she turned a corner soon after Jordan. The minute she was out of the trader's sight, Libby broke into a run.

"Where's Caleb?" she asked when she caught up to Jordan. Jordan tipped his head toward a store.

"Find him!" Libby commanded. "Hurry!"

When Jordan stepped inside the store, Libby followed a few moments later. Near the front were several people. Caleb stood with them, as though waiting to talk to the storekeeper.

When Caleb saw Libby and Jordan, he walked to the back of the store where there weren't any people. Libby hurried after him while Jordan took a different aisle.

"Caleb," Libby whispered when she reached him.

A frown crossed his face. "What are you doing here?"

"There's something you need to know."

"Go back to the *Christina*. You can't follow us."

"Riggs is outside," Libby answered as Jordan joined them.

"Riggs?" Jordan's eyes widened.

Caleb wasn't so quick to believe Libby. "Are you sure?"

"I wouldn't forget that man for anything."

"Then tell me what he looks like." Caleb sounded as if he still didn't trust her.

Kneeling down, Libby pulled out pencil and paper and used the floor to make a sketch. With quick sure strokes she drew the tall hat, the deep lines of the man's face, then his cruel eyes.

"That's Riggs, all right," Caleb said.

"And look!" Libby pulled out the reward notice.

As Caleb read the notice, Jordan watched the front door. "There he is!" Instantly Jordan turned his back to Riggs.

"Keep down, Libby," Caleb warned. "Follow me." As though nothing were wrong, Caleb walked along the aisle until he stood behind a pile of high boxes. Libby crawled after him.

When Jordan reached the boxes, he, too, was hidden from Riggs. As Caleb dropped to his hands and knees, Jordan did the same. Together the three of them crept down the rest of the aisle and around the corner. Halfway into the next aisle, they came to the back door.

Still crawling, Caleb pushed open the door and slipped through. Jordan and Libby were right behind.

Once outside, they started running. Down one block, then up another. Through a backyard into another street. More than once, a dog barked or a cow mooed. But Caleb kept on, climbing the steep hills of Burlington until Libby was out of breath.

By the time Caleb paused, they had made so many twists and turns that Libby no longer knew where she was. When she started to speak, Caleb pulled her between a barn and a shed. Jordan slipped into the shadows beside them.

Moments later, running footsteps passed them on the street. Jordan peeked out. "It's Riggs."

"Let's double back," Caleb whispered as the footsteps faded away.

When Jordan nodded, the two boys moved as one person, with Libby following. Through the back alleys they ran, this time downhill. Within a block or two, they changed directions. The muscles in her legs aching, Libby followed them through a ravine and up a steep hill.

When Caleb finally stopped, they stood at the back door of a large white house. Quickly Caleb knocked with an unusual pattern of raps. When there was no answer, he knocked again, using the same raps. It was a signal, Libby felt sure. Could she remember it?

A moment later, the door opened. As Libby hurried inside,

she glanced back. Just across the yard was a barn. Had someone slipped around a corner?

I imagined it, Libby decided. *With all the turns we took, how could anyone possibly follow us?*

Inside the house, a woman led them through a hallway. After the bright sunlight, Libby's eyes needed to adjust to the dimmer light. But Caleb walked as if he knew every step of the way.

"Why are we here?" Libby whispered.

"To see Pastor Salter."

"Who's he?"

"He used to be my pastor," Caleb told her. "When we lived in Burlington, we went to the Congregational church."

"So he's against slavery," Libby blurted out. "Is that where you learned to hate it?"

Caleb shushed her. "You talk too much."

The woman led them into a room filled with books. An east window overlooked the city and the river.

When Pastor Salter welcomed them, his face seemed warm with interest. Caleb introduced Libby and Jordan.

"Well, Caleb," the pastor said as they all sat down. "I haven't seen you for some time. How are you?"

As though talking with an old friend, Caleb grinned. "Still going up and down the Mississippi. Still finding things to do."

He tipped his head toward Jordan, and the Reverend Salter seemed to understand. "Were you followed?" he asked.

Caleb nodded. "By a slave trader, Jordan's owner. We might have slipped him, but I'm not sure. If he knows you, he'll know where to look."

A smile lit the pastor's eyes. "Yes, he'll know where to look."

As Caleb told the story, Pastor Salter listened intently.

"If your mother came through here, I haven't seen her," he told Jordan at last. "Do you want Caleb to go to Salem for you?"

Jordan shook his head. "If he finds Momma, she'll be feared to trust him."

"It's very dangerous for you to go," the pastor warned.

"The Lord, He go ahead of me." A light shone in Jordan's black eyes, as though he felt no fear.

"Yes," the pastor answered, as though he, too, felt sure of that truth. "And you, Libby? Are you going with them?"

Libby glanced at Caleb, expecting him to say no. Instead, Caleb said, "If you want to go, I'll take you."

"You'll take me?" Libby felt surprised. *Maybe Caleb trusts me, after all,* she thought.

Then Caleb explained to Pastor Salter. "We don't think the slave trader saw Libby. But if he follows her now, she'll lead him to the *Christina.*"

Libby's hopes shattered into a million pieces. *So you're afraid I'll give you away, Caleb Whitney. You still don't trust me!*

Auntie Vi's words haunted Libby. *I'm ready to give up on that girl,* she had said. *Did Caleb feel the same way?*

Then Pastor Salter cut into Libby's thoughts. "We've had so much traffic lately that one of my members is in the barn right now. He has a load of seed potatoes you can deliver in Salem."

As though expecting such a plan, Caleb grinned.

He knows so much, Libby thought. *He has to be part of the Underground Railroad.*

"I'll have a message sent to your father," the pastor told Libby. "He needs to know what's going on. He's captain of the *Christina,* right?"

"How did you know?" Libby asked.

"I respect your father. I value him as an able captain and as a man of God."

A man of God, Libby thought. *What does that mean?* She loved her father, but the way Pastor Salter talked, it sounded as if Pa was a saint. Libby had never thought of him in that way.

"We'll need boards, sir," Caleb said, "and a hammer and nails."

"Take whatever you find in the barn," the pastor answered. "But first, I want to pray for all of you."

When he bowed his head, Libby bowed hers too. Yet she peeked. Then Caleb and Jordan closed their eyes, and Libby decided she better do the same.

In a strong voice the pastor prayed. "Lord, we ask thee to help Caleb and Jordan and Libby know the way they should walk. Give them light when they need light, and darkness when they need darkness. Clothe them with your disguise."

When Pastor Salter paused, Libby's thoughts raced ahead. *He prays as if he really expects God to do something!*

"Deliver them from their enemies," the pastor finished. "We thank thee, Lord. Amen."

"Amen!" Jordan exclaimed. "Amen, amen!" He grinned at Caleb, then at Pastor Salter.

As Caleb opened the back door, ready to go outside, Libby stopped him. "I think I saw someone as we came in," she warned. "I wonder if there's a man lurking around the barn."

CHAPTER 14

The Big Test

This time Caleb acted as though he believed Libby. Instead of walking straight to the barn, he led Libby and Jordan to the front door, then around the side of the house. There they waited and watched.

When Caleb felt it was safe, he took them to the back side of the Salter barn. When Caleb opened a door, Libby and Jordan slipped inside.

A farmer waited there, along with two horses hitched to a wagon. Caleb recognized one of the horses.

"So old Dobbin's still around!"

"He's given you rides since you were nine years old." The farmer lowered his voice. "I thought you had given up this business."

"For a while." As if the matter weren't terribly important, Caleb winked. "I look different now, don't I? Older and more mature."

When the farmer looked uneasy, Libby suspected that Caleb's change of appearance might be wishful thinking. But why was it important that he looked different? Were there people from whom he needed to hide? People who might hurt him?

Caleb went to work at once. At one side of the barn he picked up boards and a hammer and nails. He and the farmer pounded the boards together in an upside down U. Then Caleb and Jordan set the strange arrangement at the front of the wagon bed.

As though used to taking such a place, Jordan climbed into the wagon and curled up. The U-shaped frame protected his sensitive back. Caleb set down another board, and the U became a box. Then he and the farmer loaded the wagon with sacks of potatoes. When they finished, Jordan's hiding place was covered.

As Caleb and Libby climbed up on the high seat, the farmer stepped close. "I wish you weren't doing this, Caleb. Take extra care. You mean a lot to us."

The sun was slanting westward as Caleb turned the horses into the street. Though Libby had a thousand questions, she managed to stay quiet until they reached the open road west of Burlington.

She had just started to feel they had gotten safely away when she heard hoofbeats behind them. When she turned to look back, a curve in the road hid whoever followed.

Caleb clucked to the horses. As they picked up their pace, he shifted the reins into one hand. With one quick movement he pulled off his cap, mussed up his hair, and stashed the cap back on his head. When he hunched his shoulders, Caleb looked like a different person—older, thinner, not like the fun person he was.

Libby giggled, and he flashed her a grin. Yet she knew this wasn't a game.

"Look back, Libby," he said quietly. "Has anything bounced out of place? Any sack of potatoes covering the boards over Jordan? Anything that would make a slave catcher suspect him?"

Turning, Libby knelt on the seat to check every inch of the wagon bed.

"Do you hear the hoofbeats, Jordan?" she asked softly.

"Yes'm." His voice came through a small opening in the board under the backside of the seat. "Don't you worry none. I lies as still as these here potatoes."

As Libby sat down again, Jordan slid a piece of wood across the opening. Already the hoofbeats sounded closer. "Can you hurry the horses, Caleb?"

"If I push them, whoever is following will know that I've got something to hide."

When they reached a crossroad, Caleb stopped the horses and listened. Again Libby glanced around, but she saw only trees. The hoofbeats had stopped.

Caleb flicked the reins across the backs of the horses. As soon as they moved on, Libby heard hoofbeats behind them again. Though she wondered if it were her imagination, Caleb's hands tightened on the reins.

"Don't look again, Libby." He spoke in a low voice. "You have to pretend it doesn't matter."

"But it does!" she exclaimed.

"Sure, it does. But you can't act scared, or you'll give us away."

"How do I not act scared? I'm scared silly!"

"Take a deep breath and smile." Caleb took his own advice, then let his shoulders sag again.

"Caleb? Who's following?"

"One man on horseback."

"You know by the sound?"

"Yup."

"Is it Riggs?" Libby dreaded even the thought of the man.

"Don't know. But probably."

"How could he find us that easily? I didn't see anyone when we left the house."

"Neither did I. And there wasn't anyone when we left the barn. But everyone knows that Pastor Salter is an abolitionist —a person who wants to abolish slavery. If Riggs knows that, too, and he probably does—"

Suddenly Libby understood. "He would wait somewhere until we left the barn."

"Yup."

As the sun dropped behind the trees, the hoofbeats drew closer. Libby obeyed Caleb and didn't look back. But her teeth started to chatter.

"Are you cold?" Caleb asked. "Or afraid?"

"Both."

Reaching around, Caleb grabbed a blanket from on top of the potatoes. At the same time he managed to glance back.

"It's Riggs, all right." He handed Libby the blanket. "Did he see you before you came into the store?"

"I doubt it," Libby answered. "And then I was down on the floor drawing."

"Put the blanket over your head like a shawl," Caleb said. "Let it cover your dress and fall forward around your face."

Quickly Libby obeyed. The blanket's warmth felt good, and she stopped shaking. Yet her frightened feelings were growing. If someone caught them with a runaway slave in the wagon, they were breaking the law. They could even go to prison!

Closer and closer came the hoofbeats.

"He'll try to stop us," Caleb warned, still speaking low.

"Pretend that you're enjoying a nice spring ride. But let the blanket hide your face."

Soon Libby heard the hoofbeats close behind the wagon. *How can I possibly act as if I have nothing to hide?* But Caleb could, and she would have to also.

Suddenly the awfulness of it all struck Libby funny. When she giggled, Caleb spoke in a low voice.

"That's the way. Keep it up."

Libby's next laugh was forced, but it didn't sound too bad.

As she looked toward Caleb, she saw the rider out of the corner of her eye. He was even with the bed of the wagon, and they were entering a stretch of lonely woods.

"Have you noticed the sun?" Libby asked. "I've never seen a prettier sunset—all gold and pink."

Libby knew she was talking nonsense, but she couldn't think of anything else to say.

"And purple," Caleb added as the rider pulled alongside him. "It's a good time of day to be out."

Beyond Caleb, Libby saw Riggs. There was no doubt about the evil in his eyes. Libby shuddered but remembered to hide her face. Then she recalled the farmer's words. *Caleb is known to people around here. For some reason there's extra danger for him.*

Holding the blanket forward at the side of her face, Libby again forced herself to laugh. "I declare," she said. "If you haven't got the fanciest way of driving these horses!"

Just then Riggs called out. "Stop!"

"Can I help you, mister?" Caleb asked, as if aware of the rider for the first time.

"Stop and let me look in that wagon of yours!"

"I can stop," Caleb said politely. "But I want to get my friend to Salem soon."

"What have you got in your wagon?"

"Seed potatoes, sir. A right good crop."

"And you're taking 'em to Salem?"

"Yup! Folks there think the load I'm hauling is worth an awful lot."

Riggs slowed his horse. As Libby heard the hoofbeats drop back, she knew Riggs was matching the pace of his horse to that of the draft team. She had no doubt that he was staring at the bags of potatoes.

For the next half mile or so, Riggs rode just behind Caleb, staying even with the wagon bed. Not once did he speed up or slow down. It took every ounce of Libby's strength not to turn around.

Suddenly Riggs cursed. As he struck the side of the wagon with a whip, Libby jumped.

"Just wait!" Riggs threatened as he came alongside Caleb. "I'll find out what you're up to!" This time Riggs cracked the whip against his own horse. The mare leaped ahead.

As soon as the slave trader was out of sight, Caleb leaned down and knocked on the long board under the seat. When Jordan slid aside the piece of wood hiding the opening, Caleb spoke to him. "You all right, back there?"

"This here Jordan is all right." Again his voice came through the broken-out space at the back of the seat. "Was he lookin' at me?"

"Yup. He looked you over. Did you stop breathing?"

Jordan laughed. "I stopped breathin', all right. I jist got the breath of life back."

Caleb's laugh sounded as if he, too, had been let out of jail. "Glad you're still with us."

As the last rays of sun dropped below the horizon, Caleb turned to Libby. "You did a good job."

Libby felt warm with his praise. She felt even more glad that for at least this moment he seemed to trust her.

"You didn't tell a lie," she answered.

"That's what I learned from the Friends," Caleb told her.

"Friends?" Libby asked.

"Society of Friends, the Quakers at Salem. Truth telling is important to them. It's also their protection. They don't get twisted up trying to remember a lie. If a slave catcher asks a question, he knows a Quaker always tells the truth. Sometimes that truth is what throws the slave catcher off."

"I'd be so scared that I'd tell a lie," Libby answered. "I don't see how you and the Quakers do it. Especially if you're trying to hide someone from an evil man like Riggs."

In the last bit of light Caleb grinned. "Just wait. You'll see what I'm talking about."

"You are the strangest boy I ever met," Libby answered.

"Yup. I probably am." Caleb didn't seem at all disturbed by her idea of him.

"Does that bother you? Don't you care what people think?"

In answer Caleb took his gaze from the road. "I care about what some people think."

"But not everyone."

"Not everyone."

"Why?" Libby asked.

Caleb shrugged, as if his answer were as plain as day. "If I respect someone, I care about what they think. If I don't respect someone, it's not always important what they think. They might want me to do something I don't believe in."

"Like telling them where Jordan is hidden."

Libby sighed. She wished life could seem so simple to her. She could only wonder if Caleb respected her. She wanted that respect more than anything she had wanted in a long time.

Every now and then, Caleb stopped to rest the horses. Only once, when they pulled into a woods at the side of the road, did Jordan crawl out from under the sacks of potatoes and get down to stretch.

When they started out again, Libby knew what to ask. "Caleb, what do you want to be when you grow up?"

"A newspaperman." Caleb answered so quickly, there seemed no doubt in his mind.

"A newspaperman?" Libby hadn't guessed this side of Caleb. She only knew that he always expressed himself well.

"A newspaperman like Elijah Lovejoy."

Again Libby felt curious. "Who's Elijah Lovejoy?"

"An editor who died at Alton," Caleb said quietly.

"You want to *die* like him?"

"Oh no!" Caleb's impatience showed in his voice. "I want to live like him! Elijah Lovejoy edited a newspaper in Saint Louis— the *Saint Louis Observer*, it was called. He spoke out against slavery, and he had to flee to Alton. There he started over."

"With another newspaper?"

Caleb nodded. "The *Alton Observer*. He kept writing against slavery. Mobs destroyed his press three times. Friends raised money to buy a fourth press, and Elijah hid it in one of those warehouses we saw along the river. A mob gathered and shot him."

"That's when he died?"

"Yup. The mob threw his press into the river."

"Why do you want to be a newspaperman like that?" Libby asked. "It sounds like you'd be asking for a lot of trouble."

"Maybe," Caleb answered. "But what I really want to be is someone who stands up for things that are important."

"Even though you know what comes with it?" Libby asked. "You might be persecuted too."

Caleb glanced down to the hole in the back of the seat. "Even though it's dark, Jordan knows he has to hide. You don't know what he went through to escape from Riggs. He went without food and water. He hid in the bushes and risked his life."

Caleb leaned down and spoke into the broken-out space. "Tell her, Jordan."

But Jordan didn't answer. Libby wondered why. Maybe he didn't want to tell her.

"I bet he's fallen asleep," Caleb said finally. "When Jordan ran away, he knew that at any minute he could be shot or found by bloodhounds. What he did was a thousand times harder than anything I've ever done."

Farther down the road Caleb spoke again. "You know, Libby, this wasn't Jordan's first escape. He tried before and was brought back. This time Jordan was ready to die if that's what it took to be free."

"I'd be scared," Libby said. "I'm scared now, just thinking about it."

"I am too," Caleb answered. "But there's something your pa told me. 'We all have times when we're afraid. What counts is what we do, even though we're scared.'"

There was something Libby still wondered about. "When we were in Saint Louis, why did you start writing the *Christina's* name in the dirt?"

Caleb stared at her. "You don't miss much, do you? I hoped Jordan would remember the letters. It would help him find us."

"Caleb," Libby started, then hesitated. She felt afraid to ask. "Do you trust me now?"

"I think so," Caleb answered. "But don't do anything stupid. It's Jordan's freedom that's at stake. And maybe his life."

Suddenly Libby thought about what it meant to be a never-give-up family. Was Jordan now part of the bigger family Pa talked about? In everything they did, Jordan and Caleb seemed to look out for each other.

Not for anything will I do something to hurt Jordan, Libby promised herself. With all her heart she meant it. Yet a feeling of dread tightened her stomach. *What if I get so scared that I do something wrong? What if I try hard to do everything right and still give Jordan away?*

~ CHAPTER 15 ~

More Danger

By the time the moon came up, Libby's eyes had grown used to the darkness. Here and there, patches of snow lay in sheltered hollows on the north side of a woods. Whenever Libby noticed such a patch, she realized how hard it would be to hide, even at night, against that whiteness.

As they entered the village of Salem, Libby saw no one stirring on the streets. Yet Caleb seemed to know exactly where to go. When he stopped at a large barn, he jumped down and opened a large set of double doors. As soon as he led the horses and wagon inside, he closed the doors.

Libby thought Caleb would let Jordan out of the wagon right away. Instead, Caleb went quietly to work, unhitching the horses.

"Where are we?" Libby asked in a low voice.

"Henderson Lewelling built the house where we're going," Caleb whispered. "But he doesn't live there anymore."

"It's a Quaker family?" Libby asked.

Caleb nodded. "Amos and Ellen Kimberly."

When Libby tried to ask more questions, he whispered, "Shhhhh!"

Within the wagon box Jordan lay without making a sound.

Working quickly, Caleb took the harness off the horses and rubbed them down. Not until he had given them hay and hung the harness on hooks did Caleb return to the wagon. Standing next to the load of potatoes he spoke softly. "Stay there, Jordan. I'll make sure it's okay."

To Libby it seemed a long time before Caleb came back. When he returned, he pushed back the U-shaped box.

"It's safe, Jordan," he whispered. "C'mon out."

Like a giant figure rising from a mountain of potatoes, Jordan stood up. When he jumped down from the wagon, he moved stiffly. On the ground he flexed his muscles, then followed Caleb and Libby from the barn.

Outside, Caleb led them through a back street, then an orchard, to a side doorway in a large stone house. As if someone had watched for them, the door swung open from the inside.

When it closed again, the person lit a candle. To Libby's surprise the person was a boy. Caleb introduced him as Samuel.

"Wast thou followed?" Dressed in the plain Quaker style of work pants and homespun shirt, Samuel seemed about their age.

"Right outside of Burlington," Caleb said. "He left us, but I think he'll be back."

"Then come!" Samuel motioned to Jordan.

In the kitchen Samuel pushed aside the table and a braided rug. As he opened a trapdoor, Libby saw a crawl space large enough to hide several people under the floor. When Jordan stepped down into it, Samuel whispered to him, "We'll give thee food as soon as it's safe."

Samuel and Caleb closed the trapdoor and replaced the

rug and table. Moving quickly, Samuel set bread, cheese, and a pitcher of milk on the table. While he dished up soup from a kettle on the wood cookstove, Libby looked around.

Heavy curtains were drawn against anyone who might look through the windows. Only one candle lighted the room.

"I need to talk to your father," Caleb told Samuel.

As though it wasn't at all unusual to wake someone at such an hour, Samuel left to get his father.

Caleb was still eating when Mr. Kimberly came into the kitchen. "We welcome thee," he told both Caleb and Libby as he sat down at the table.

"I'm looking for a woman named Hattie Parker," Caleb said. "She might have had three children with her."

Mr. Kimberly shook his head, but then Caleb named a place in northeastern Missouri.

This time Mr. Kimberly nodded. "I know it."

As Caleb leaned forward, the light of hope lit his face. "So you've seen the woman I mean?"

"No," Mr. Kimberly answered. "But I've seen a young woman from the same place. Her name is Emma. She came alone."

"No one else was with her?" Caleb sounded puzzled.

"Emma had a desperate time. Someone else had planned to run away with her, but she was forced to leave alone. She even had to leave her three-month-old baby."

"Her *baby*?" Libby blurted out.

"Emma could barely speak of it," Mr. Kimberly told her. "I don't know what happened that her escape plan went wrong. She had no choice but to keep coming. On the smaller rivers she crossed on the ice, but the Des Moines River was breaking up."

"Where is Emma now?" Caleb asked.

"I sent her to Denmark."

"A town close to the Iowa border," Caleb explained to Libby. "Asa Turner's town. Remember when I told you about him?"

Libby remembered, all right. Father Turner wanted the men who came to Iowa to choose wives who felt proud to wear a jean dress or checked apron. In Saint Louis Libby had bought her jean cloth, but she hadn't finished sewing her skirt.

Caleb turned back to Mr. Kimberly. "You sent Emma to Deacon Trowbridge's house? Maybe she could tell me more about Hattie Parker."

"I believe thee might learn—"

In that instant a loud knock sounded on the back door. Caleb's quick glance searched the room, as though making sure nothing would give them away.

"Go into the dining room," he told Libby. "Take your dishes along. Stay out of sight."

As Mr. Kimberly walked slowly to the door, the knock changed to a loud pounding. Standing in the dining room, Libby watched Caleb through the doorway into the kitchen.

Still holding his glass of milk, he tipped back his chair. For all the world it looked as if Caleb were just having a late-night snack.

Moments later, Libby heard the door open. "Good evening, friend," Mr. Kimberly said. "What dost thou want?"

"An escaped slave who entered your house."

Libby recognized the voice. *Riggs, there on the doorstep!* Filled with dread, she stepped back, farther into the dining room.

"He's a tall boy," Riggs said. His voice sent shivers down Libby's spine. "About fifteen, sixteen years old."

"I have been asleep in my bed," Mr. Kimberly answered. He sounded as calm as if he met such a cruel man on his doorstep every day. "I saw no slave enter my house."

"I'll search," Riggs said, his voice bold. "I'll find him."

"My wife and son are in their beds," Mr. Kimberly answered. "Thee must not frighten them."

Frantically Libby looked around the dining room. All she could think about were the evil lines in the slave trader's face and his cruel eyes. *Where can I hide?*

Then she glanced back through the doorway to the kitchen. Looking as calm as he had on the road, Caleb was still eating.

"I know you!" Riggs said suddenly.

Caleb tipped his head, as though politely saying hello. "We met on the road."

"No! Somewhere before!" Riggs answered.

But Mr. Kimberly spoke again. "Thee hast no search warrant. I wish thee good night."

To Libby's surprise she heard the firm closing of the outside door. Riggs was shut out, and she was shut in! Yet when Libby returned to the kitchen table, she found herself shaking.

Once more Mr. Kimberly sat down. Across the candlelight he faced Caleb with a stern look in his eyes. "Why hast thou taken a chance by coming to Salem?"

With respect Caleb listened, honoring his host.

"It is dangerous for thee to come here!"

Caleb nodded. But when he answered, he sounded years older than he was. "You have learned, my good Friend, that we don't always choose which dangers we want."

For a long moment Mr. Kimberly's gaze met that of Caleb. Then he glanced toward Libby. "And this friend thou hast brought with thee?"

"Libby is new to our ways," Caleb said.

Libby wondered if he was warning the Quaker gentleman about her. *You can trust me!* she wanted to cry out. *I won't give away your secrets!*

But Caleb gave her no chance. "Will you forgive me for bringing danger to your house?" he asked Mr. Kimberly.

The man's slow smile reached even his eyes. "Forgive thee for doing the Lord's work? There is no need. But I feel concerned for thee and for thy grandmother."

"You are right to feel concerned," Caleb answered. "I do too."

Another long look passed between them. Then Mr. Kimberly reached out to lay his hand upon Caleb's. "I will pray daily for thy protection."

When Caleb spoke again, it was to ask for fresh horses.

"I will do my best for thee, but I cannot promise. Our need is great right now. Can thou walk if thou must?"

Caleb nodded. "We'll leave as soon as it's dark again."

As Libby listened to them talk, she washed up the dishes. Already she was learning. Not a dish could be left that would give away extra visitors. But there was something else she had discovered by watching Samuel. *If a slave catcher asks Pa whether he's seen a fugitive, he can honestly say no. It's Caleb who usually sees them. It's Caleb who takes care of them.*

For the first time Libby understood the relationship between Caleb and her father. *Without talking about every fugitive who comes, Pa agrees with what's happening. Caleb knows him so well that he knows Pa approves.*

When Mr. Kimberly left them, Caleb set a bowl of soup, bread, cheese, and a glass of milk on a tray. Quickly he moved the table and rug and opened the trapdoor. Jordan blinked up at them from the dark hole beneath the floor.

"C'mon," Caleb whispered. "Riggs is through searching for a while. You'll be more comfortable in the basement."

Libby followed the boys down the steps to a room with a fireplace. As though Caleb had often been there before, he started the fire.

"You'll be safe here now," he told Jordan.

Sitting cross-legged, Jordan devoured the soup and sandwiches. When he finished eating, he lay down between the blankets left for whatever fugitives came to the house.

As Libby and Caleb returned upstairs, the morning sun crept above the horizon. They found Mrs. Kimberly in the kitchen. She gave Libby a Quaker bonnet and told her to use it later. Then she led Libby upstairs to her own bedroom.

"Thee may rest here," she said.

Mrs. Kimberly had put clean sheets on the bed, and Libby sank down into them. She had time for only one or two thoughts about the Lewelling and Kimberly families and all the people who had passed through this house. Then Libby turned over and fell asleep.

When she woke, she felt strangely mixed up. Was it the gray light just before dawn? Then she realized a day must have passed.

For a few minutes Libby lay there, remembering all that had happened. The longer she thought about it, the more scared she felt.

What will we find out about Jordan's mother? she wondered. Why is it dangerous for Caleb to come to this small town in Iowa?

～ CHAPTER 16 ～

The Hiding Place

As night covered the land, Libby and Caleb again ate in the kitchen. Libby felt sure that it was Mrs. Kimberly who cooked the good food. Yet she was nowhere in sight when Samuel took food to the basement for Jordan.

In the darkness before the moon came up, Caleb and Jordan slipped outside. Carrying the bonnet from Mrs. Kimberly, Libby followed the boys. As they passed through the orchard, Caleb often stopped in the shadows under the trees. More than once, he looked around and listened.

By the time they reached the barn where they had brought the horses, Libby felt like a shadow. Already she had learned to slide in and out of whatever building she entered.

Behind her, not even the barn door creaked. Were the hinges well-oiled for times like these?

The horses and wagon they had used the night before were no longer there. Instead, a fresh team of horses stood hitched to a wagon filled with hay. To Libby's surprise, both Caleb and Jordan burrowed under the hay.

"Put on thy bonnet," whispered a man wearing Quaker garb.

When Libby tied the strings beneath her chin, she knew

that the deep brim hid her face.

The elderly Quaker motioned her toward the high front seat. As soon as she sat down, he opened the doors of the barn. Quickly he led the horses out, shut the doors, and took his place beside Libby. When he flicked the reins over their backs, the horses moved into the street.

As the wagon rolled out of Salem, Libby felt surprised by the warmth of the night. After the chilly days on the *Christina*, the warmer temperature felt good. When they were safely out in the country, their driver told Libby what to do.

When they reached the village of Denmark, Iowa, the elderly Quaker stopped his horses near a stone house on the edge of town. Following his instructions, Libby walked up to the door.

"A friend of mine needs to see you," she said to the woman who answered her knock.

"Then bring him at once," the woman answered.

When Libby returned to the wagon, the boys slid out from under the hay and hurried to the door.

When Caleb lifted his cap, the woman saw his face. Here, too, he was known.

"Come in quickly," she said, and they all slipped inside.

"We're looking for Emma," Caleb whispered to Mrs. Trowbridge.

With light, quick steps she led them up a flight of stairs. At the top was a children's bedroom lit by one candle. Near an opening along an outside wall sat a black girl not much older than Libby.

Emma's hair was cut short and curled close to her head. Holding her arms as though hugging herself, she swayed back and forth.

"Emma," Mrs. Trowbridge said gently.

As the candlelight fell upon the girl, Libby saw her lips moving. Drawing closer, Libby heard the words. Soft and low, Emma repeated them over and over.

"Lord Jesus, Jesus! I asks you for my baby. Jesus!"

Afraid to break into the girl's prayer, Libby waited. But Jordan knelt down in front of Emma.

"Emma," he said softly.

She seemed not to hear. Still swaying, she kept on praying. "My baby, Jesus. My baby."

Jordan raised his voice. "Emma!"

This time she heard. As though coming back from a distant place, her eyelids slowly lifted. Her large black eyes looked deep and troubled.

"Jordan?" she asked. "Jordan Parker? You still in this world?"

Jordan's rich laugh filled the room. "Yes, I still in this world. And so is you!"

"But not my baby!" The sorrow in Emma's voice cut like a knife. "I ain't got no idea where little Henry is!"

Mrs. Trowbridge knelt down next to Jordan. On her knees she leaned close to Emma's face, as though wanting her full attention.

"Remember what the deacon said?" Mrs. Trowbridge asked, as if she had told Emma many times.

"Tell me please. Tell me again."

"He said, 'Any mother has the right to keep her baby.' And do you remember what he did? He strapped on his six-shooter. He mounted his horse, and he left."

"To find my baby. It was night, black night, when he left. Why ain't he back?"

"Deacon always does his best with whatever he does," Mrs. Trowbridge told her. "This is the second night, but you have to give him time. You need to eat and sleep."

Emma shook her head. "Not till my baby is in my arms."

"I want you to eat," Mrs. Trowbridge said. "And Jordan has some questions for you."

Mrs. Trowbridge handed the bowl of soup to Jordan, then moved back. When Mrs. Trowbridge left the room, Emma once more closed her eyes. As if trying to shut out her pain, she swayed back and forth, praying.

Jordan set down the bowl but stayed on his knees in front of the girl.

"Emma!" His voice was sharp. "Hear me now! The Lord, He done heard your prayers!"

Emma stopped rocking. Her eyes opened. "He did?"

"He did!" Jordan told her again. "Now you jist begin thankin' Him!"

"Jordan? You lie to me?"

"Has I ever lied to you before?"

Slowly Emma shook her head. "Back on Old Massa's plantation you done speak the Lord's words. When my husband ran away, you told me big Henry be safe in Canada. And a man wrote a letter that say big Henry is!"

A light broke over Emma's face. "If you tell me my baby is safe, I believe you, Jordan Parker! I believe you cuz you knows the Lord!"

Closing her eyes again, Emma lifted her arms toward heaven. "Glory! Thank you, Jesus!"

Tears blurred Libby's sight. Emma seemed like a new person.

"Oh, Lord!" She was wailing now. "You brought us out of Egypt!"

"Thank you, Lord!" Jordan joined her. "These arms—these arms will hold her baby again!"

Suddenly Libby felt scared. How could Jordan make such a promise? What if he were wrong? Emma's grief would be even greater.

But Emma had no doubt as to whether Jordan spoke the truth. Suddenly she lowered her arms and opened her eyes. Reaching out, she picked up the bowl of soup. "I will eat so I be strong when I holds my baby!"

Taking the spoon, Emma lifted it to her mouth, as if she hadn't eaten for days. When the bowl was empty, she handed it to Jordan. As though no one else was in the room, she spoke directly to him. "But I ain't got good news for you."

Jordan leaned forward, hanging on to every word.

"When Old Massa sold your momma and me, we made big plans. We plan to follow the North Star to the peoples with broad-brim hats. We plan to cross over the Jordan to the Promised Land."

As though not wanting to say more, Emma stopped.

"Go on, girl!" Jordan exclaimed.

"Your momma and me—we planned to leave together. Together we has four good hands and four feets. Together we could take your sisters and your brother and my baby. With four hands and four feets we sure could reach the Promised Land."

"But what happened?" Jordan asked, as though not wanting to delay the bad news any longer.

"On the night we planned to run, I took everything I has—" Emma held up a big handkerchief tied into a bag. "I went to your momma's cabin. I was in the cabin when a poundin' come on the door. I crept back in the corner and hid in the dark. Man at door say, 'That girl Emma, she's run. You git up to the Big House, Hattie. Massa want to talk with you.'"

"And then?" Jordan asked.

"He drags your momma out of the cabin and don't see me there in the corner. When they left, I knows I couldn't go back to the Big House. They would beat me and—" Emma groaned. "I crept through the dark—through the dark to the cabin where my baby was. White man stand there at the door. A man waitin' for me."

Emma didn't need to finish. Jordan bowed his head, hiding his face within his arms.

"Momma?" he asked at last. His voice was muffled. "What happen to Momma?"

"I don't know." Emma spoke slowly. "I think she be working at the Big House."

"And Serena? My sister Serena? My brother Zack? And baby Rose?"

"With your momma, I think." For a time Emma sat quietly, as if she could say no more.

Then Jordan asked, "How does I find the place where Momma is? What did you see on the way here?"

When Emma told Jordan everything she remembered, she said, "I was goin' to help your momma with my extra hand. Your momma can't cross the rivers alone—not with three young'uns."

Suddenly Jordan's strong shoulders trembled. Great sobs rose from deep within. As he tried to hold them back, his body shook. Only one sound escaped his lips—a moan of pain.

When at last Jordan raised his head again, his face held no trace of tears. A strange new look—a strength that Libby didn't understand—seemed to glow through his brown skin.

Jordan wasn't seeing her or Caleb. He wasn't even seeing Emma. Instead he looked up, raising his face to heaven.

"Let my momma go!" he pleaded. "Let my people go!"

~

When Mrs. Trowbridge returned, she had more food—this time for the rest of them.

Jordan ate hungrily, as though planning to store up for a long time. When he finished, he eased his body against the wall. His long legs and bare feet stretched out in front of him.

With his head back against the wall, Jordan closed his eyes. At first Libby thought he had fallen asleep. Soon she knew better.

When Jordan opened his eyes, he spoke to Caleb. "I is goin' back," he said. "I is goin' back for my momma and my sisters and my brother Zack. I is goin' to be my momma's hands and bring them out."

"You can't go," Caleb said. "Not now."

"Not now? I has to go. The longer Momma stays—"

"Every slave catcher in the country is looking for you. You've got a two hundred dollar price on your head! They all want that reward!"

"I take the swamps. I take the woods."

"Those slave catchers are crawling all over the swamps and woods, just seeing if they can find you under a rock!"

"I be under a rock, all right!" Jordan looked directly at Caleb. "And not one of them men will find me!"

"You can't go back," Caleb told him again.

"I will," Jordan said. "I has to."

"Not now." Caleb's blue eyes met Jordan's strong brown gaze. "If you do, everything you've done by escaping will be lost."

"Momma told me I would lead my people out. The good Lord told me I would lead my people out."

"You will, Jordan," Caleb answered. "But it has to be when God tells you to go. Is He telling you now?"

Jordan groaned. "Why you have to bring the Lord into it? It's me tellin' me to go. It's my worry for Momma and my sisters and my brother that's tellin' me to go."

Again Jordan groaned. But he said no more about leaving that night to find his family.

When Mrs. Trowbridge came for the dishes, she showed Libby the hiding place at one side of the bedroom. Just under the roof the narrow room stretched from one end of the house to the other. Though only three or four feet high, it had enough space to hide several people.

On her hands and knees, Emma crept into one end of the hiding place. Jordan and Caleb crawled into the other end. Mrs. Trowbridge pushed blankets into the opening, then told Libby what to do.

"Our children usually sleep in this bedroom, but they're gone tonight. Keep the entrance to the hiding place open to let in the heat. But close it up the minute you hear someone knock on the door downstairs."

Across the front of the opening, Mrs. Trowbridge set two small boards. At the top of each board were heads of nails pounded though the wood to look as if they were nailed into something. Yet one nail was loose. Mrs. Trowbridge used it to hold the boards, then set a shelf in place.

On the shelf Mrs. Trowbridge put three books. When she moved back, the combination of boards and shelf became a built-in bookcase.

After making sure that Libby knew what to do, Mrs. Trowbridge opened the hiding place again. "The heat from our stove will come right up the steps," she said. Again she left for downstairs.

As Libby lay down on the bed, she felt sure she would never fall asleep. Worry filled her mind, scattering her thoughts every which way.

If someone knocks on the door, Mrs. Trowbridge needs to answer. What if a slave catcher comes with a search warrant? What if he runs up the steps before I get the shelf in place? What if I can't remember how to do it?

Libby's fingers shook, just thinking about it. She dreaded the sound of loud knocking on the door. She hated the thought of quickly lighting a candle and closing up the hiding place.

Then something else bothered Libby even more. *Why does Caleb need to hide? He's not a fugitive. Or is he?*

Yet in the deep darkness before dawn it wasn't pounding on a door that woke Libby up.

~ CHAPTER 17 ~

Skunk River

In the dark, early morning hours Libby heard hoof-beats coming closer, still closer. As the hoofbeats stopped next to the house, Libby felt something creep past the spot where she lay.

"Who's there?" Libby cried out.

"Emma!" a voice answered.

Together Libby and Emma crawled toward the stairway. At the top of the steps they waited. Without making a sound, they listened.

The outside door opened and closed. Then a baby's voice whimpered.

Emma leaped up. "It's my baby!"

As she raced down the stairs, Libby followed close behind. Only one candle lit the room at the bottom. In that light Libby saw a man place a bundle of blankets in Emma's arms.

"My baby!" she cried. "Little Henry!" As though she would never let him go, Emma clutched the bundle to her chest. Crooning softly, she rocked back and forth.

Suddenly she stopped. Her eyes wide with fear, Emma knelt down and laid the baby on the floor. Frantic with haste, she pulled aside the blankets, as if wondering whether she had the right child.

At last she saw her baby, dressed only in a diaper and a cotton shirt. Emma stared at his face. Quickly she checked each hand, each finger, each foot, each toe. Then she rested back on her heels.

Instead of fear, her face shone with love. "You is mine, little Henry—and you is *good*!"

Gently she folded a blanket around the baby. Layer by layer she wrapped him, leaving only his face uncovered. Then she gathered him into her arms and put her face close to his.

Once again she began to rock, swaying from side to side. For Emma there was no one else in the room.

By now Caleb and Jordan had joined them. Deacon Trowbridge led his wife, the boys, and Libby to the kitchen table.

"Slave catchers are close behind me," the deacon warned. "If the baby cries, they'll hear him, even from the hiding place."

"We'll leave right away!" Caleb exclaimed.

Again Libby felt surprised by the quickness with which Caleb made up his mind. But Mrs. Trowbridge moved just as fast. Without another word, she started making sandwiches.

"My horse is worn out," Deacon said. "I'll see about other horses."

But Caleb stopped him. "Not with the warm weather we've been having. I'm hoping the Skunk River will still be frozen."

Deacon rubbed his chin. "It's smaller and more shallow than the Mississippi."

Caleb nodded. "But if we took horses and a wagon we might go through the ice."

"You're sure you want to walk?" the deacon asked. "It'll be hard with the baby."

"I'd rather cross on foot," Caleb told him. "We have a better chance of not falling through."

"You'll cut across country?" Deacon's eyes were dark with concern.

"They'll watch every road," Caleb answered. "If we leave right now, we'll be deep in the woods before first light."

On four pieces of cloth, Mrs. Trowbridge set down the sandwiches and added apples and cheese. Gathering up the corners, she tied each cloth into a bag.

Quickly she wove a long strip of cloth through the knot. As she tied the lunch around Libby's waist, she explained. "Your hands will be free if you need them."

As they stood at the door, ready to leave, Deacon Trowbridge warned them. "Don't try to hide in the house," he said, as though knowing where Caleb would go. "It's being watched."

Caleb grinned. "Just take care of the dogs."

Dogs? Libby shivered. *We'll have dogs following us?*

She couldn't think of anything more frightening. Unless it was a dog like Samson, that is. Samson wouldn't hurt even a flea on his own back. *Maybe Caleb is teasing.*

But then Libby remembered the dogs she had seen from the Burlington hotel. She was starting to put two and two together, and she didn't like the answer she got.

In the darkness before dawn they set out—Caleb first, then Emma and the baby, Libby, and finally Jordan. Past the town square and the Denmark Academy they walked. Past the houses they crept, making no sound. When they reached the north side of the village, Caleb slipped between trees still bare of leaves.

He seemed to follow a path, but Libby could not see it. Then, as the darkness gradually faded, she noticed a faint pressed-down line of grass. Before long, even that disappeared. This was no ordinary trail marked for everyone to see. Only a bent twig here or there helped the person who knew how to look.

Ahead of Libby, Emma's bare feet passed over the cold earth without sound. Behind Libby, Jordan also walked with bare feet. Between the two of them, Libby felt strangely cared for—as though the desperate experiences they had known would now protect her.

More than once she wondered if she would be able to keep up. Both of the boys were in good shape. The fast walk through the woods seemed no problem to them. Not even Emma with her baby lagged behind. Her step seemed light, as if she carried no extra weight.

They were well into the woods when Libby heard dogs barking from somewhere behind. Emma flinched and started to run.

Libby whirled around, but trees blocked her view. Instead, she saw Jordan—calm, strong Jordan with a bead of sweat above his lips. With fear in his eyes, he, too, was moving faster.

But Caleb only turned his head, as though making sure they all followed. "It's all right," he said quickly. Though he picked up an already rapid pace, his movements showed no fear.

Libby strained to listen. Her heart was still pounding when she realized something had changed. From behind she heard no barking dogs. No dogs moved closer and closer.

When she glanced around, Libby knew that Jordan had also heard the change. As he hiked through the woods, a smile played around his lips.

Libby had no idea how far they had walked when Jordan suddenly passed her. With great, long strides, he caught up to

Caleb. Reaching out, he put a hand on Caleb's shoulder.

As Caleb turned, Jordan held a finger to his lips. "Shhhh!" he seemed to say.

With quick movements of his hands, Jordan motioned them off the path. Into the trees he led them as he seemed to search for a hiding place. When he came to a thick tangle of bushes, Jordan took them to the far side, then stopped.

"What's wrong?" Caleb whispered.

"The Lord, He warned me," Jordan answered. "He say, 'Watch the river, Jordan. There's danger at the river.'"

"Did the Lord tell you what to do?" Caleb asked, as though he had no question about Jordan's ability to hear God.

In the gray light before dawn a grin spread across Jordan's face. "I 'spect He talk to you 'bout that."

Libby could barely hear Caleb's low laugh. Yet the strangeness of it shocked her. How could they make a joke out of what seemed to be terrible danger?

For a minute Caleb stood there, as though thinking about what to do. "We're almost at Skunk River," he said finally. "It could be Riggs. If he figured out that we went to Denmark, he'll know we need to cross the river to reach Burlington. He'll know there's no bridge. And he'll know the best place to cross."

"And if it's not Riggs?" Libby asked.

"The men who followed Deacon Trowbridge could be following us—without their noisy dogs."

Which is it? Libby felt scared, just thinking about it. *Riggs ahead of us? Or slave catchers behind?*

Then fear tightened Libby's muscles. *Or is it both? We could be caught in between!*

Caleb looked as calm as if he did this kind of thing every day.

"Remember Pastor Salter's prayer?" he asked. "That we would know the way to take? We're going to try a different crossing."

And Pastor Salter prayed something else, Libby remembered. *Give them light when they need light, and darkness when they need darkness.*

As though hearing Libby's thoughts, Caleb spoke again. "The sun will soon be up. If there's ice, we go across on the river. If there's not—"

Caleb's hands tightened, as though dreading the thought. "There's a small boat upstream from where I'll bring you. It's hidden under the bushes next to the river."

He turned to Emma. "If we get separated, you and Libby go ahead. Cross the river and keep going till you come to a farm. Don't go near the house. The man who lives there is being watched. Hide in the trees behind the barn, and we'll meet you there."

"And if you can't?" Libby asked. She didn't want to think about the possibility.

Caleb's strong gaze met Libby's. "If we can't, Emma will know what to do. If Jordan and I don't find you before dark, don't wait for us."

"Don't wait?" Libby whispered. "If you and Jordan get stopped, what will you do?"

Caleb shrugged. Without answering, he turned away. As they started out again, he did not return to the path, faint though it was. Always, he walked around any branch that would snap. Always he circled any pile of leaves from last autumn—leaves that might rustle with dryness.

Then, just ahead, Libby saw the edge of a bank. Caleb dropped onto his stomach and wiggled beneath the branches of a patch of bushes. Carefully he looked every which way.

Before long, Caleb backed out from the bushes. Leaning close to Emma and Libby, he warned them. "Right here the bank is really steep. In fact, it's a nine- or ten-foot drop. No one will expect you to cross."

In the early light of dawn Libby saw that the ground fell sharply away. Then came the river.

"The ice is holding," Caleb whispered. "If we cross now—"

Libby knew what he meant. Even in an hour, with the warming of the day, the ice could give way.

"You go first," Caleb told Libby. "Let Emma pass down the baby. When Emma gets below you, lower the baby to her."

Already Emma was working quickly, reshaping the bundle of blankets. When she finished, Libby saw that in the outermost blanket Emma had tied a handle. To that she knotted another blanket, this one stretched full length, like a rope.

"Don't wait for us," Caleb told Libby again. "Whatever happens, you and Emma keep going."

As Caleb held her hand, Libby slipped over the edge of the bank. When she felt around for a foothold, her feet sank into snow where the sun's rays did not reach.

Emma's bare feet! Libby thought in the moment before she started sliding.

Frantically she reached out, caught a branch, and hung on. But the branch snapped, and Libby slid farther. In her downward plunge, she again reached out. This time she grabbed the trunk of a small tree.

Libby had barely caught her breath when Emma called to her. "Ready?" she whispered, as though unmoved by the danger.

Digging her feet into the snow, Libby braced her body

against a larger tree. "Ready!" she whispered back.

Carefully Emma lowered the blanketed baby. Slowly she let out the line, letting the slippery snow carry the baby down.

Just before little Henry reached Libby, the line gave out. With shaking hands Libby climbed up, took hold of the bundle, and hung on.

Making her own new path, Emma slid down the hill past Libby. At the edge of the river, Emma braced herself. With her heart pounding again, Libby lowered the baby to Emma.

"I gots him," Emma whispered at last. For an instant she gathered the baby in a grateful hug. Then her hands moved swiftly, rearranging the blankets again.

This time she pulled out two long corners. Slinging one corner over her shoulder, she pushed the other corner under the opposite arm. Reaching back, she tied the two ends. With little Henry safely cradled in front of her chest, Emma's hands were again free.

At the shore of the river, Libby stepped down, expecting to find ice. Instead, cold water rose around her feet. Suddenly she yelped.

"Hush!" came the quick warning from above.

Libby leaped from the water to a foothold in the bank.

Just then a voice cried out. "Over there!" a man shouted.

"Get him!" called another.

The slave catchers! Like the cold water, terror washed over Libby.

In the woods above, a branch snapped. Pounding feet seemed to shake the earth as the boys drew the slave catchers away.

"You told the catchers where we is!" Emma's whisper was sharp with anger.

Libby's terror changed to panic. Guilt weighed her down. *What will happen to Caleb and Jordan? What will happen to us?*

"The ice—" Libby whispered, unable to think of what to do. In the stronger light the ice looked mushy and soft.

"We is goin' anyway!" Emma tested her footing.

In those few minutes the gap between the river bank and the ice seemed to have widened. The cold, dark water waited for one wrong step.

As Libby tried to plant her feet, she slipped in the soft ground. Before she could cry out, Emma clapped a hand over her mouth.

"From now on, I is leadin' you!" she exclaimed in an angry whisper. "And you listen up!"

With her baby close to her chest, Emma crouched next to the water. Again Libby struggled to find her footing. Just then she heard a sharp cry. Turning, she looked up.

A man's face peered over the steep bank.

"There they are!" he cried. "I found them!"

～ CHAPTER 18 ～

Trapped!

In the next instant Emma leaped. Her bare feet found the ice, then slid. But she kept her balance and started running.

Close behind, Libby also leaped. When she stopped sliding, she raced after Emma.

The ice felt soft, as if it would give way at any moment. Ahead of her, Emma started a zigzag path.

Why doesn't she go the shortest way? Libby wondered.

Unwilling to follow, she headed straight for the far shore. Suddenly Emma called to her. "Thin ice!"

Just in time, Libby saw a patch of ice blacker than the rest. Sliding to a stop, she barely escaped crashing through.

Libby needed no other warning. She, too, started to zigzag. In the growing light she followed the white and stronger ice.

Once she turned for a quick look. In that moment a man slid down the steep bank behind them. A slave catcher!

With all her strength, Libby raced on. When she looked again, the man was gaining on her. Even in the midst of her fear he looked familiar.

Desperately, Libby stared at the ice ahead. A large fallen tree hung over this side of the river. *If I cut across that stretch—* But Emma had gone around.

Then Libby saw it. Black ice again. Thin ice, that meant. Libby heard a warning crack.

Again she followed Emma, instead of taking the shortcut. A minute or two later, Libby heard another crack. A man cried out.

This time Libby stopped. Close to the fallen tree, the slave catcher struggled in open water. Waving his arms, he cried for help.

For an instant Libby wondered what to do. Then as the man reached up, he managed to grab a branch and hang on.

Near the shore Libby again leaped an expanse of black water. Already Emma was climbing the straight-up-and-down bank on that side of the river. Libby followed, clinging to every handhold she could find.

Partway to the top, she looked back at the slave catcher. Using the branch of the fallen tree, he had managed to pull himself onto the trunk.

"He'll ice up," Libby called to Emma. "He can't follow us."

"Someone else kin," Emma called back. "Hurry up!"

Someone else. Before they started this wild race, Libby had heard at least two voices. Where was the other slave catcher?

Out of breath now, Libby panted as she climbed the rest of the way. Where were Caleb and Jordan? Had the other catcher caught them?

It's my fault, Libby thought. *I promised myself I'd never give Jordan away. But that's what I did. I gave everyone away!*

At the top of the riverbank, Emma paused for just one moment.

"You saved my life!" Libby exclaimed as soon as she caught her breath. "I would have fallen right through those thin spots!"

As though it weren't important, Emma shrugged.

"I mean it!" Libby said. "Thank you!"

Emma simply turned and started on.

She's putting up with me. Again Libby remembered how she had given the rest of them away. *Emma knows she'd be better off without me.*

Suddenly Libby recalled Auntie Vi. She had tried hard to be a good mother, but she hadn't always done the best thing. For the first time Libby could understand that. *At least Auntie tried.*

Again Emma walked so fast that Libby found it hard to believe that she carried a three-month-old baby. As Libby tried to keep up, she felt more miserable by the minute. *Maybe Auntie would like to know how I am. Maybe I should write and tell her. That is, if I ever get back to the boat!*

With each step, water sloshed inside Libby's shoes. In the morning air her feet felt painfully cold, then numb. Yet Emma walked without any shoes at all. Watching her, Libby felt ashamed for wanting to complain.

Caleb's directions brought them to a wooded ravine. As they climbed between the steep hills, Emma turned and looked back. Then, as if satisfied that no one followed, she walked on.

Hollows in the ravine still held patches of snow. Each time Emma came to one of those patches she walked around it. Careful to follow her example, Libby kept away from anything that would leave a footprint for whoever searched.

By the time they reached level ground, Libby was shivering. But Emma walked on, her bare feet seeming to fly across the cold earth.

When Libby finally saw a farmhouse, she wanted to run

to the door, knock, and be let in. But Emma stayed within the line of trees until she reached the barn. Then she walked farther into the woods. There she found a fallen log and sat down.

It was warmer there, out of the March wind, and Libby pulled off her wet shoes. She had just settled herself when she heard a whisper.

"C'mon," Caleb said. "We have to keep going."

"You're here!" Libby exclaimed, then clapped a hand over her mouth. Her relief had startled her into speaking aloud.

Though Libby could see no trail, Caleb hurried all of them on as though he knew every bush.

"How far to Burlington?" she asked him once.

"Nine, maybe ten miles from the farmhouse."

Deep in the woods, Caleb finally allowed them to stop. Only then did the girls find out what had happened. When Caleb and Jordan drew the slave catchers away, both men followed them at first. Then one dropped back, deciding it was better to guard the river.

"When he fell through the ice, the other man went to help him," Caleb said. "The second slave catcher built a fire, and guess who showed up?"

Libby didn't have to be told. "Riggs?"

"Yup. We saw them talking. Jordan and I kept to the woods on the south side of the river. We crossed farther on."

Suddenly Libby realized why the slave catcher seemed familiar. "That's the man who talked to Riggs outside the store in Saint Louis! So Riggs pays him for this?"

"'Fraid so," Caleb answered. "Riggs probably sent the catcher to wherever Jordan's mother is. It would make sense that Jordan would go there."

"And the other catcher?" Libby asked.

"Someone looking for Deacon Trowbridge and the baby."

"And me," Emma added.

"Whoever the catchers are, they're greedy for money," Caleb said.

"Do you think we've gotten away from all of them?" Libby asked.

"Nope. If we stay in the woods, they won't find us, but they'll guess where we're going. If the slave catchers hire horses, if Riggs doesn't spare *his* horse—"

Dread tightened Libby's stomach. "They'll be waiting for us to come into Burlington."

"Unless we beat them there." Caleb stood up. Once again he led them on.

Libby wasn't sure when she felt as if she couldn't walk any more. Perhaps it was when the blisters formed on her feet. Or when her wet shoes seemed too heavy to lift another step. Whenever it was, Libby's entire body hurt.

"Can't we wait till dark?" she asked Caleb.

He shook his head. "That's what everyone does. And you're forgetting something. Your pa needs to leave Burlington tonight. We *have* to get back."

Somewhere in the miles after that, Libby grew ashamed. Jordan looked as though he had just begun his walk and could go for miles more. Emma was no different. She was headed for the Promised Land.

Even Caleb seemed used to such a long hike. As they drew close to Burlington, he suddenly stopped. Libby dropped down on a stump, feeling she would never be able to move again. Caleb shinnied up a tall tree.

From there he gazed out over the countryside. But Libby needed no long view to hear a galloping horse. The thunder of hooves told her more than she wanted to know.

Caleb slid down from the tree. "It's Riggs! He's headed straight for Pastor Salter's barn!"

Using a shortcut, Caleb led them through a wooded ravine. When at last they came to the back side of the barn, Libby felt she had never seen anything so beautiful in her life.

As soon as they stepped inside, Caleb dropped down a wooden bar to lock the doors. Moments later Libby heard the rhythm of hooves on the street alongside the barn. Closer and closer the horse came. Suddenly the sound of hooves stopped.

"It's Riggs," Caleb reported from his lookout at a window. "He's standing in the trees back of the barn."

Before long, Libby heard other horses. From a window on another side, Jordan made his report. "Two slave catchers here!" They, too, stood just inside the line of trees.

"We're surrounded?" Libby asked Caleb.

"Riggs is watching the door where we came in. The slave catchers are guarding the big door. If we used the third door— the one toward the house—we'd get the Salter family in trouble."

Libby's stomach tightened. Just when she thought they were nearly safe, everything got even worse. How could they possibly get back to the *Christina* without being seen?

Feeling hopeless, she dropped down on a mound of hay. Nearby, Emma found another soft place. From the handkerchief bag she carried, she pulled out a diaper and changed little Henry, then began to feed him.

As minutes ticked away, Libby grew more and more nervous. "Do you think Pastor Salter knows the men are here?"

"Nope," Caleb answered. "All of them are standing out of sight from the house. And the Salters have no way of knowing that we're back."

"What are the slave catchers waiting for?" Libby asked.

Caleb wasn't sure. "They might think we're still coming. I took every shortcut I know."

"And Riggs?"

"Maybe he's waiting for dark. Or maybe he has more men coming, men who will help him make sure we don't get away."

Libby shivered. Either way, they would lose.

Whenever little Henry whimpered, Emma rocked him. Each time she stood up to walk back and forth, she seemed more afraid.

Libby felt as if a clock ticked louder with every passing minute. *How long can Emma keep the baby quiet?*

When Caleb gathered all of them into a part of the barn away from windows, Libby again sat down beside Emma. "Has your husband ever seen your baby?" she asked.

"Jist once he seen him. The night little Henry was born, big Henry crept into my cabin. 'Glory!' he say. 'What a son!'"

Tears filled Emma's black eyes. "That night big Henry gots to run from Old Massa."

"Is your husband in Canada now?" Libby asked.

Emma nodded. "When we gits to the Promised Land, this baby will sure nuf know his daddy!"

"We need a plan," Caleb said suddenly. "A bold plan. Everyone knows that fugitives move at night. That's what both Riggs and the slave catchers expect. We need to do something they won't expect."

Jordan caught on at once. "We needs to move before dark."

"In broad daylight?" For Libby sneaking around in the night was difficult enough.

"We can't wait for dark," Caleb said. "It's bad enough having three men out there. We can't take a chance on more. Somehow Jordan and Emma and Henry have to get to the *Christina* without being seen."

"But how?" Libby asked.

"One of us has to walk out past Riggs and the slave catchers," Caleb answered. "Walk out in a way that they don't recognize what we're doing."

"Them catchers knows me," Emma said. "Young Massa hired one of them. And they knows my baby!"

"That Riggs!" Jordan exclaimed. "If he don't know my face, he sure do know my back!"

"Well, Caleb," Libby said. "I guess it's your job to go."

But Caleb was silent. When he did not answer, Libby remembered.

"Why did that farmer warn you? And that Quaker in Salem? Why is it dangerous for you to be in this area? Do all the slave catchers know you?"

"They know that wherever I am, there will probably be a fugitive with me. They want to stop what I'm doing."

And still you do it! Once Libby would have wondered why Caleb got involved. Now she thought she knew.

When the silence stretched long between them, Libby looked from Caleb to Jordan to Emma.

It was Caleb who spoke. "Libby—"

"You don't have to tell me," she said. Each time Riggs came near, Caleb had protected her. He had kept the slave trader from seeing her face. Even the one slave catcher who followed her across the river had seen more of her back than her face.

"If we could get the baby past them—" Caleb said.

"Just the baby?" Libby asked.

"If he cries, he'll give everyone else away."

"So you want me to take the baby?"

Caleb nodded. "If you do, the rest of us have a better chance of sneaking out."

"But how can I keep him quiet?"

"By rockin," Emma said. "He like rockin' best."

"Rocking in front of Riggs and the slave catchers? How can I do that?"

Again Libby looked from one to the other. No one answered.

"You saw the men talking," she told Caleb. "If I carry a baby, all three will know where it came from."

Then Libby looked at Emma. She sat on a mound of hay again, cradling her sleeping baby. With the blankets pushed aside, Libby saw little Henry's long black eyelashes and his curly hair. In peace he slept, as though no danger could possibly touch him. But if Emma had to walk—

Suddenly Libby had an idea. "Rocking—but not in my arms. What about rolling in a wagon?"

Emma didn't understand, but Caleb did. "A wagon pulled by a Newfie!"

Libby explained to Emma, then asked, "Would it work?"

"Maybe," she answered. But she wasn't sure.

"I could climb out a window—" Libby looked toward Caleb.

He nodded. "Riggs is at this end of the barn, watching the door we came in." Leaning down, Caleb drew in the dirt floor. "The catchers are over here, guarding the big door. If you went out the third door they'd see you go to the house. But you could climb out this window. Walk this way—"

Caleb raised his head to look into Libby's eyes. "You might get close to the street before Riggs sees you. If it's just one person, he might not catch on."

"I could get Samson." Libby planned it out. "I could pretend I'm bringing laundry to the Salters. I would stop here and take the baby."

Suddenly the idea of what she'd have to do seemed more frightening than she could handle. "What if it doesn't work?"

But Caleb was already making plans. "Libby, do you know the way back to the *Christina*?"

"We ran so fast that I didn't notice directions."

"Then I'll show you." Again Caleb took up the stick and drew in the dirt. "This is where we are—"

Soon his lines became streets. Before long, those streets led to the river. "Cross Hawkeye Creek here. All you have to do is get to the *Christina* and find help."

"What if Pa isn't there?" Libby asked.

"Ask Gran," Caleb said. "She'll tell you what to do."

"And if she isn't there?"

"Talk to Osborne. He's *always* there."

Libby still felt shaky. Her part in the plan seemed very simple in comparison with what Jordan and Emma had already done. Yet Libby could not push her terror aside.

After all that has happened to Emma, what if I lose her baby?

CHAPTER 19

Samson's Disguise

"Libby?" Caleb broke into her thoughts. "You better get moving."

Slowly Libby stood up. She walked over to the milking stool that Caleb set beneath a window. Her panic-filled thoughts darted in every direction. *I gave them away once. What if I do it again?*

Yet there was more. More, even, than the failure Libby dreaded. In just a few hours she had come to know Caleb and Jordan and Emma better than any of her Chicago friends. Together the four of them had faced life and death.

Are they part of my never-give-up family? Libby wondered. *What if something happens and I never see them again?*

Next to her stood Caleb, the strange boy that she now admired. The boy who stood up for what he believed but who was, after all, just as much fun as any other boy.

Before his honest gaze, Libby knew she also had to be honest. If she didn't, there was something that would always stand between them.

"I need to tell you something," she began. "I'm sorry for the things I said when I first came onboard the *Christina*."

Caleb's glance toward Jordan and Emma told Libby that he knew exactly what she meant.

"I forgive you, Libby," he said. "If Jordan and Emma knew, they'd forgive you too."

But Libby wasn't satisfied with that. *If I want a never-give-up family, I have to be that kind of person.* Leaving the window, Libby walked back to the others.

"Jordan—" she stopped.

Somehow Jordan knew, knew that she had never cared enough to find out what was happening to his people.

"Sometime I tell you, Libby," he said. "I tell you how I escaped."

But it was Emma that Libby worried about most of all. Dropping down, Libby tried to see into her eyes. "Do you trust me, Emma? Do you trust me with little Henry?"

At first Emma did not look at her. When at last she lifted her gaze, her eyes still looked dark and scared. Then she spoke. "I trusts you, Libby. I trusts you with my baby."

"You're sure, Emma? What if something goes wrong?" Libby dreaded even the thought.

"You be a right fine conductor, Libby. You won't lose your passenger."

"But I'm *scared*!" Libby wailed. "I can't do all the things the rest of you do! I can't walk through swamps, or talk to slave catchers, or forgive someone who beats me. I can't—"

Caleb stopped her. "Libby, just do what's in front of you."

"Caleb?" Libby still didn't feel sure about this prayer business. But if it might help—"Caleb, will you and Jordan and Emma pray for me?"

Caleb nodded. "The whole time."

"I mean now," Libby said.

"I like Pastor Salter's prayer," Caleb answered. He bowed

his head. "Lord, help Libby to know the way she should walk."

As she heard Caleb's voice, Libby felt strangely moved. Talking to God like that seemed so—so safe.

"Give her a disguise," Caleb went on. "Deliver her and us from all our enemies."

"Amen!" Jordan prayed.

"Amen, amen!" Emma whispered.

But will it really work? Libby wondered. *Will that prayer work for me?*

Again Caleb looked out one side of the barn. The slave catchers were still there, staring into the ravine as though expecting someone to appear at any moment.

Jordan looked out the other side. Close to the trunk of a tree, as though trying to stay out of sight, Riggs waited.

"I'll come back with my dog," Libby promised Emma. "Have little Henry ready when I come."

Once again Caleb helped Libby climb onto the milk stool. As she took hold of the windowsill, Caleb remembered something else. "By the way, you should know that Mr. Bates is a Southern sympathizer."

"Mr. Bates?" Libby stared at Caleb. "The first mate of the *Christina*? You mean if he had to choose, Mr. Bates would be on the side of a slave catcher?"

"Maybe."

"He'd help Riggs?"

"Maybe. Just don't trust him."

Outside the window there were bushes. Beyond them, a dirt street. *If I can just reach the street, if I can just walk away—*

As Libby climbed through the window, she felt glad she no longer wore a fancy dress. When she dropped to the ground,

her heart pounded. Quickly she looked around, sure that anyone within miles could hear. But no slave catchers, not even
Riggs, peered around a corner.

Libby straightened. Brushing back her hair, she pulled up
her Quaker bonnet. After smoothing her skirt in place, she
took one deep breath and started walking.

When she reached the spot where Riggs could see her, Libby
did not change her pace. Nor did she look around. Trusting
that the deep brim of the bonnet would hide her face, she kept
her back to the slave trader.

Without turning her head to the left or the right, Libby
walked. With her shoulders back and her step confident, she
walked. As though life was simple and never dangerous, she
walked as Caleb had told her. Only when she felt sure she was
hidden by a hill did she dare look back.

When Libby was sure that no one followed, she broke into
a run. Soon great ragged breaths tore her chest, and she had to
stop. Yet before long she hurried on again.

After the miles she had already traveled that day, the six
or seven blocks to the river seemed to take forever. When
Libby staggered up the gangplank, Samson stood at the top, as
though she had just left him. Seeing Libby, he wagged his tail
until it should have fallen off.

"Good dog!" Libby said quickly as she hurried past him.
With new energy, she headed for her father's cabin. As though
unwilling to let her out of his sight, Samson followed close behind. But Captain Norstad wasn't there.

Libby raced to the pastry galley and learned that Gran
was shopping for groceries. And when Libby searched out Osborne, he, too, had gone into Burlington.

Once again, Libby's heart filled with fear. *Is there anyone else I can trust? I should have asked Caleb.*

As she tried to decide what to do, Samson's tail slapped against her. At last Libby noticed.

"You poor dog!" she exclaimed. "After being gone three days I don't even pay attention to you!" Kneeling down, she stroked his back, then scratched behind his ears.

But Libby's stomach was doing flip-flops. "We're on our own, Samson," she whispered in his ear. "I just wish there were someone who could help!"

Just then Libby heard a voice behind her. "Is there something I can do for you?"

"Yes, I need—" she started to say. Then she looked up. *Bates! The first mate!*

For the first time since Libby had known him, he sounded helpful. Then Caleb's words leaped into her mind. *He's a Southern sympathizer.*

With growing panic, Libby scrambled up. "I need—" Suddenly she hiccuped loudly.

Mr. Bates stared at her. "You need what?"

Libby held her breath. But when she opened her mouth to speak, she hiccuped again.

"Don't say it, young lady. You need a glass of water!"

Libby nodded. The moment Bates asked a waiter for water, Libby fled.

The pastry galley was filled with the aroma of freshly baked mince pie. Libby quickly found a laundry basket and a large tablecloth. On the main deck she searched out the wagon. Her fingers fumbled, but at last she had Samson's harness just right.

I'm ready! Libby thought. *No, not quite.* Riggs and the slave catchers would never expect a fugitive to wear a fancy dress.

Libby snatched up the basket and raced back to her room. There she opened the tablecloth and used it to line the basket. Inside that, she set a pair of shoes. Throwing open her trunk, she found gloves, then searched out a piece of thin cloth she could use for a veil. With great long stitches, she sewed the veil to the brim of her Quaker bonnet.

Now, a dress for Emma. Which one would be best?

They were almost the same size, and Libby pulled out one dress, then another. None of them seemed right. Finally she came to the pale green dress that she liked most of all, the dress that reminded Libby of her mother.

When I wore this dress, Auntie Vi and Uncle Alex thought I looked beautiful. Even my friends said so. This is the dress I'll wear when I want to look my very best.

Then Libby remembered. *It's a little bigger around the waist for someone who's just had a baby.*

For one moment Libby stroked the pale green cloth. Then, before she could change her mind, she folded the dress and laid it inside the basket.

With her fingers flying, Libby changed into another dress and a bonnet of her own. With all her heart she hoped to pass for someone different from the person who walked away from the barn.

On the main deck again, Libby set the laundry basket in the wagon. As she snapped a leash to Samson's collar, Bates spoke from behind.

"Here's your water, Miss."

This time Libby put on the smile she had practiced in front of a mirror. "Thank you, Mr. Bates."

With one gulp she drank the water, then said, "I'll just take Samson for a walk."

Down the gangplank they went, with Libby taking the lead. When they reached the landing, Samson walked beside her, as if they had done this a thousand times. Wherever he went, the wagon trailed behind.

Up the hill Libby and Samson walked, back over the streets to the Salter barn. Whenever Samson seemed unsure about what to do, Libby lifted the leash and gave a slight tug on the collar. Samson understood where she wanted him to go.

By the time they drew close to the Salter house, the sun had dropped behind the trees. Were the men still there, waiting for dark? If they were, there was little time left.

Libby's hands turned clammy. With every part of her being she wanted to run. But an idea entered her head. *What would I do if my mother were a washerwoman?*

Suddenly Libby knew. As though she had no other thought than to deliver clean clothes, she walked to the side door. Raising her hand, she pretended to rap.

For a few minutes she stood there, as though waiting for an answer. When none came, Libby walked boldly toward the barn. Still on the end of the leash, Samson followed with the wagon.

"Anybody home?" Libby called out.

Inside the line of trees, the two slave catchers still waited. As Libby glanced that way, they stepped out of sight. If Libby hadn't known they were there, she would have missed them.

"Anybody home?" Libby called again as she walked to a window of the barn. Again Samson followed. Standing on tiptoes, Libby peered in.

As though still searching, she walked to the largest door of the barn. When she tried the door, she found it unlocked. Opening it wide enough for Samson to follow, Libby walked through.

Caleb stood waiting in the shadows. With one quick movement he lifted the clothes from the basket. Gently Emma placed her baby inside. Loosely she drew the cloth together.

"Is Riggs still there?" Libby whispered.

"Still there," Caleb said softly. "We'll sneak out as soon as we can."

"Come on, Samson," Libby called as she walked back outside. With her hand still on the leash, Libby started toward the street. Then she had another idea.

"Let's try the house again," she said to Samson in a voice she hoped the slave catcher could hear. She hoped, too, that Caleb still watched from inside the barn.

This time Libby rapped softly, using the pattern she had heard from Caleb. Almost at once Mrs. Salter answered.

"I have a laundry basket here," Libby said. Quickly she picked it up.

Surprise flashed through Mrs. Salter's eyes, but her voice was warm with welcome. "Come in, come in!"

The moment Libby stepped into the kitchen she spoke quietly. "Two slave catchers and a slave trader are watching your barn. Caleb and the others can't walk out in front of them."

"I see." Mrs. Salter smiled. "I wonder if the three gentlemen would like to have supper. Especially if I serve it out of sight from the barn? On the front porch, for instance?"

Libby grinned. "I'm very sure they must be hungry."

From inside the basket little Henry cooed. Reaching down,

Mrs. Salter pulled aside the cloth, then the blankets. "What a precious bundle you're carrying!"

Gently she replaced the blankets and tablecloth. As Libby left the house, she felt warmed by Mrs. Salter's smile.

Setting the laundry basket into the wagon, Libby spoke to Samson. "C'mon, boy. C'mon." With a slight tug on his collar she led him away.

But Libby was nervous again. She had only one thought: "If I can just get Henry to the *Christina* before he starts crying!"

CHAPTER 20

The Never-Give-Up Family

Down the long streets to the river Libby walked with Samson padding faithfully beside her. By the time they reached the *Christina*, night had fallen around them. The lantern near the gangplank welcomed Libby home.

Quickly she took the harness off Samson. When Libby picked up the laundry basket, the dog followed her to the texas. Inside her room Libby pulled the blankets to one side. Henry lay fast asleep!

For the first time in years Libby breathed a prayer of thanks. But then she wondered, *What will I do if Emma doesn't come soon?* She had no idea how she would feed a baby.

From the window of her room, Libby watched for shadows on the landing. Finally she saw them. Three shadows crept along the warehouse where the men had hid that first night.

This time Libby knew who belonged to the shadows. Hurrying out of her room, she shut the door behind her. All the way down the flights of stairs, she watched for Bates. Outside the large main cabin she nearly ran into him.

Libby caught her breath. "Good evening, Mr. Bates," she said.

"Good evening, miss," he answered.

Suddenly Libby had an idea. "Mr. Bates, did you know that Caleb's grandmother made your favorite mince pie this afternoon?"

To Libby's surprise his thin lips parted in a smile. "Why no, I didn't. Thank you for telling me." Turning, he started toward the pastry galley.

Libby grinned to herself. *If there isn't anyone to see him, he'll eat a whole pie! How much time will that give us?*

The moment the first mate was out of sight, Libby raced down to the forward deck. Lifting the glass of the lantern, she blew out the flame.

Near the gangplank, she waited. On his haunches beside her, Samson waited too.

Moments later, Libby heard soft steps running up the gangplank. As Emma reached the railing, she glanced back, as if to see whether she were followed.

Then Libby stepped out to welcome her three new friends. Up the stairs to the texas she and Emma flew. They found little Henry opening his eyes.

Sweeping the blankets aside, Emma picked him up. Holding him close to her face, she spoke. "Little Henry, you is goin' to see your daddy! And when you gits to Canada, you is *free*!"

Looking up at his mother, the baby waved his arms.

Emma laughed. "See what a smart boy I gots? He knows what his momma tells him, all right!"

Once again, Emma wrapped the blankets around the baby. This time she held him out to Libby. Taking little Henry, Libby cradled him in her arms.

"How did you get away from the barn?" she asked.

Emma's grin reached even her eyes. "That lady—that missus in the house—you know what she done? She ask them three men watchin' us if they want supper. 'Yes, ma'am!' they say.

"'Well, then,' the missus say. 'You come round to the front porch.' When they was sittin' there gobblin' up their food, why, we snuck out!"

Libby giggled. "It worked!"

"Caleb he say we have to leave right now," Emma went on. "I change clothes as fast as I kin."

"Change?" Libby asked. "Oh no! I want you to wear that dress. You still have a long way to go before you reach Canada."

Emma stared at her. "You wants me to wear this?"

"I hope it's your disguise," Libby answered. "Did you see how nice you look?"

When Emma's black eyes met the eyes of the girl in the mirror, surprise passed over her face. As if unable to believe the dress was really hers, Emma's hand slipped down between the folds of the skirt. Slowly she stroked the beautiful cloth.

When she looked up, her gaze met Libby's. "I ain't got nothin' for you."

Then suddenly Emma reached for Libby's scissors. With great care she cut a lock of curly hair from baby Henry's head.

When she laid the scissors down, Emma turned to Libby. Carefully she placed the black curl in the palm of Libby's hand.

"I thanks you," Emma said simply.

Libby knew that she meant much more than the dress.

∾

As the oil lamps on the *Christina* flickered out, deck-hands lowered the yawl hanging over the stern into the water. As though nothing important were happening, one of them rowed the small boat to the river side of the *Christina*.

While Libby, Captain Norstad, and Samson watched from the hurricane deck, Caleb stepped into the yawl. Moving as nimbly as a cat, Emma followed him. When she sat down, Jordan passed her what looked like a laundry basket filled with blankets. Emma set the basket next to her feet.

As Libby leaned over the rail, Jordan stepped back, then disappeared. *Where did he go?* she wondered. *I still want to find out how he escaped from Saint Louis.* Then Libby remembered her father warning Jordan to stay out of sight when in port.

When Caleb dipped the oars into the water, Libby's hands tightened with nervousness. Out in the open river someone could easily spot them. Not even Bates could eat pie forever! What if Riggs or the slave catchers appeared at just the wrong time?

As Caleb's strong arms pulled the oars, the yawl skimmed away from the *Christina*. Just before Emma disappeared in the darkness, she looked up. Searching out Libby with her eyes, she waved, then Emma and little Henry escaped into the night.

"Will they be all right?" Libby asked her father.

"I believe so," he answered. "It's too dangerous to send the baby on a train."

"Caleb will take her to the closest station?" Libby's voice was little more than a whisper, and she didn't mean an actual train station.

When her father didn't answer, Libby remembered. *I shouldn't have asked.* In spite of all the things that they could talk about, there were things she must learn not to say.

But then Pa looked down and smiled. "It's good to have you back, Libby. I'm very glad that you're safe."

"So am I!" It still seemed unbelievable that everything had worked out.

"I guess that's part of being a never-give-up family," Pa said. "We like being together." Stretching out one of his long arms, he gave her a hug.

A smile played at the corners of his mouth. "Libby, I strongly suspect that you have become a railroad conductor."

Looking up, Libby felt overwhelmed by the way Pa loved and accepted her. She wanted to tell him how much that meant to her. Instead, she could only say, "I strongly suspect you are right."

Just then she heard footsteps behind them. "You wanted me, sir?" asked Mr. Bates.

"I have some things we need to talk about," Captain Norstad answered. "Let's go to my cabin."

As Mr. Bates passed through the doorway, Libby's pa turned back. One eyelid dropped in a long, slow wink.

Libby almost laughed out loud. Just in time she clapped a hand over her mouth.

Soon Libby's laughter died. With growing nervousness she waited for Caleb to return. Finally, after what seemed like hours, she heard the quiet dip of oars.

Libby raced down the stairways. By the time she reached the main deck, Caleb had come alongside.

His grin warmed her, and so did his words. "Let's tell Jordan what happened," was all that he said.

As Libby followed Caleb to the engine room, her thoughts leaped ahead. In just a few short days, her life had changed forever. Libby knew she would never again be the same. *What will happen next? Where will we go? What will we do?*

She felt sure that wherever the *Christina* took them, it would be exciting.

**Don't miss the next
Freedom Seekers book,
*Race for Freedom!***

A shadowy figure lurks on the dark riverfront near the *Christina.* Libby Norstad is sure that it must be the cruel slave trader Riggs, who has vowed that no slave of his will ever escape alive. Does Riggs suspect that the runaway Jordan Parker is hiding on her pa's steamboat?

Fearful that Riggs may try to board the *Christina* in disguise, Libby and her friend Caleb scan the crowds of passengers bound for Minnesota Territory. Has Riggs slipped by unnoticed? Because of fugitive slave laws, he can bring Jordan back into slavery even from a free northern state. Can Jordan manage to escape discovery?

Study Guide

*A*s Libby looks down from a hotel room to her father's steamboat, a shadow separates from a building off to the right. A second shadow, then a third shadow follows. Suddenly the quiet night explodes with barking dogs . . . bloodhounds!

Hi Friends—Welcome aboard! Can three men racing toward the steamboat find freedom?

By now you may be well acquainted with the *Christina*. Or you may live close enough to a river to be able to see a similar steamboat. If not, turn to the drawing at the front of the book. As Libby goes from one deck to another, check out their names and notice the stairways between them. Soon you'll feel as much at home on the *Christina* as Libby, Caleb, and Samson.

Let's Talk About . . . Words you might need
    Find a dictionary and fill in the rest of this boat language:
Bow:
Stern:
Paddlewheel or **Paddleboat:**
Sidewheeler: Steamboat with two wheels, one on either side of the boat. The *Christina's* name is on the wood housing that protects the wheel.

Sternwheeler:

Lines:

Levee:

Decks, starting at river level:

   main deck:

   boiler deck: Just above the large boilers that heat water into steam to run the ship. Most of this deck has a railing around an open walkway. The stairs from the main deck lead up to that walkway and the large main cabin where guests and crew gather to eat.

   hurricane deck:

   texas deck: The captain's cabin and directly behind is Libby's cabin.

Now let's travel back to 1857. Use the blank space between questions to write your answers or create sections in your loose-leaf notebook when you want to write more. To find something in the story, check the number (ch. 1) at the end of the first question. That means chapter 1. Look there until you see another note (ch. 2, or 3, or 4) directing you to a different chapter.

Let's Talk About . . . The story

- How would you describe Libby at the beginning of this novel? (ch. 1)

- Why does her pa, Captain Norstad, want Libby living on the *Christina* again?

• Libby wants something she cares about more than anything. What deep hurt has made her feel that way?

• What does it mean to Libby to be part of a never-give-up family?

• What does a never-give-up family mean to her pa?

• At the end of the first chapter Pa mentions a boy who works on the *Christina*. Why does Caleb already seem important?

• What big problems does Libby face when she leaves a mansion to live on a steamboat? (ch. 2)

• Why do you think Caleb keeps Libby from snooping around the big box? (ch. 3)

• How does Caleb keep from answering Libby's questions? What secret is he hiding?

• Captain Norstad wants Libby to have a Newfie. Why? But how does Libby feel about it?

• If you don't know a Newfoundland, you might be able to get acquainted with one through a pet store or a chapter of Newfoundland owners near you. www.newfoundland dogs.com. Warning: It's hard to not bring a Newfie home!

Let's Talk About . . . Conflict

- In what we would now call homeschooling, Captain Norstad begins talking about a fugitive slave law passed in 1850. How did people in northern states handle what the law asked them to do? (ch. 4)

- What causes the disagreements between Caleb and Libby? (ch. 5) Take sides. One of you on his side. One on hers. Talk about what's going on in their world.

- Sparks fill Caleb's eyes. "You think that being treated well makes up for being *owned*?" When they reach St. Louis, where does he take Libby? Why? (ch. 6)

- What is the crack in Libby's armor—the place where she realizes what is happening to Jordan?

- How did Caleb protect Libby when she could have been badly hurt? (ch. 7)

- When Libby changed her dress and hairstyle, what did those changes symbolize?

- In what ways did Jordan remind Libby of royalty? How could someone who was a slave remind her of a king?

- What has Libby learned about her father's purpose in life? How did he live that purpose?

- What does it mean to have a purpose in life?

Let's Talk About ... Freedom ...What is it?

- Does being a freedom seeker mean that you can do anything you want? Give reasons for your answer.

- How did runaway slaves find their way at night? (ch. 8)

- When Libby was curious, Gran told her, "To understand Caleb you have to understand what he believes in." What *does* Caleb believe in? Why?

- What are Caleb's reasons for the way he answers Libby's questions? Are they good reasons or wrong? Explain.

- How did Jordan act when his leg irons were off? (ch. 10)

- Libby thinks, *Jordan is safe now.* But what would be the cost if the wrong person found him? Talk about the obstacles Jordan still faces.

- If the wrong person learned that Captain Norstad hid a runaway slave what might happen?

Let's Talk About ... Relationships

- What does Libby mean when she tells herself, "*I didn't know that being a never-give-up family would cost so much*"?

- Why does Caleb not trust Libby? Would you trust her? Why or why not?

- What important quality is at the center of Pa's relationship with Caleb? What is a code of honor?

- What happened to Libby when she saw the whip marks on Jordan's back? (ch. 12)

- What did Jordan's daddy teach him about forgiveness? How did Jordan choose to forgive?

- What happens to us if we hate someone?

- Why was Jordan free, even though he was a slave?

- What did Jordan's mother promise him? Why did her promise give Jordan a sense of purpose?

- Why were the words "Let my people go!" important to long-ago Israelites? (Exodus 7:14–16)

Now—think about Jordan crying out—*Let my people go!* Sing with them!

Let's Talk About . . . Making choices
- Pastor Salter was the real-life pastor of the First Congregational Church in Burlington, Iowa. What bold prayers does he pray in this story? (ch. 13)

- How did Jordan, Caleb, and Libby hide their identity? (ch. 14)

- If you were in the wagon when Riggs rode up, what would be the hardest part for you?

- Who are the Society of Friends, also known as the Quakers? Why is truth so important to them?

- How did Caleb tell the truth when Riggs asked, "What have you got in your wagon?"

- When Libby and Caleb are scared, he tells Libby something her pa said: "'We all have times when we're afraid. What counts is what we do, even though we're scared.'" Have you had a time when you were scared and made an unwise choice?

- Have you had a different time when you were scared and did the right thing?

- What did Samuel do so that his father could honestly say, "I saw no slave enter my house"? (ch. 15)

- Why did Libby suddenly understand the relationship between Caleb and her father?

- When Mr. Kimberly told Caleb it was dangerous for him to come to Salem, what did Caleb answer?

- When Caleb asked, "Will you forgive me for bringing danger to your house?", how did Mr. Kimberly answer?

Let's Talk About . . . God's leading

- What did Jordan tell Emma? Why did she believe him? (ch. 16)

- What is the difference between God telling us to do something and ourselves telling us to do it?

- When Jordan gave a warning, Caleb asked, "Remember Pastor Salter's prayer?" As Caleb remembered those words, how did he know what to do? (ch. 17)

- In what ways was Emma stronger than Libby in a time of danger? How did Emma know where it was safe to cross? (ch. 18)

- Who has become part of Libby's never-give-up family? (ch. 19) In what ways has Libby changed since the beginning of this book? What kind of person was she at the beginning? What kind of person is she now?

- Why did Libby ask forgiveness of each person before she left the barn?

- Caleb told her, "Libby, just do what's in front of you." What did he mean?

- How did Caleb pray for her? Why does it seem safe to talk to God the way Caleb did?

Let's Talk About . . . Digging deeper
Different fugitive slave laws were passed at different times. Look under *Fugitive slave laws* in an encyclopedia such as *World Book* and read about a clause in the Northwest Ordinance of 1787. Read about another fugitive law passed in the Compromise of 1850. What demands did such laws make?

- To see a recovered steamboat in the *Christina's* time, see www.1856.com for the steamboat *Arabia* at Kansas City, Missouri.

Let's Think About . . . Possible field trips
- **The George M. Verity Riverboat Museum, Keokuk, Iowa** www.geomverity.org Wonderful photos of various areas in a genuine steamboat along the Mississippi River.

- **Steamboat Arabia Museum, Kansas City, Missouri.** www.1856.com See a steamboat and artifacts resurrected and restored from a wreck in the Missouri River.

- **National Mississippi Riverboat Museum and Aquarium, Dubuque, Iowa** www.mississippirivermuseum.com Large complex at Tri-city hub along the Mississippi River.

Because of the time lapse between my visiting a place for research and your possible trip please check these sites online and/or by phone for more information before traveling there.

Let's Talk About . . . Your own writing

- **Talk and write about how these laws affected runaway slaves in different areas.** How did these laws also affect the people who wanted to help runaway slaves?

- What did Captain Norstad mean when he said that a fugitive slave law passed in 1850 was a bad law? (ch. 11)

- **Think about an area of the Underground Railroad that especially interests you.** What would you like to learn more about? Research this important movement and report what you find.

Jordan escaped once . . . but will he need to escape again? What will the Freedom Seekers do about it?

Thanks for being my friends through books. I'll meet you in the next Freedom Seekers novel . . . *Race for Life!*

A Few Words for Educators

Dear Parents and Educators,

The six novels in The Freedom Seekers series offer an excellent way to gain a national view of the political climate in 1857. In that critical period in American history, steamboats carried immigrants to newly opened land. Rivers were the highways of the time and the mighty Mississippi was a well-traveled route. In spite of danger, injustice, and the possible loss of all they had, people of many faiths, rich and poor, slave or free, worked together for what they believed about the rights and freedom of individuals. In life-or-death situations children, teens, and adults built the Underground Railroad.

As I returned to this series to write study guides I was struck by the similarities between then and now. Though we are a vital part of the electronic age with its countless breakthroughs, some things have not changed—the need to value and uphold our American freedoms. The need to cherish human life. The need to stand for what we believe. **Even as we had overcomers then, we have Freedom Seekers now.**

The Freedom Seekers series also offers tools for teaching topics that help our growth as individuals. Libby, Captain

Norstad, Caleb, Jordan, and their friends face questions still crucial today:

- Who can I trust?
- What do I *really* care about?
- What does it mean to be a never-give-up family?
- How can I live out my belief in the freedoms sought in the Declaration of Independence and the Bill of Rights?
- In what ways do I need to recognize the Lord's leading in both daily and life-or-death situations?
- What practical skills should I develop?
- Why do I need to put my faith in God?
- How can I live with biblical principles and values?
- How can I make choices based on those principles and values?
- And how can I encourage others to do the same?

The Freedom Seekers series weaves together fictional characters with carefully researched people who lived or were known in 1857. Each novel stands alone but is best read in sequence to see the growth of characters and relationships. A new character, Peter, who is deaf, joins the *Christina* family in the fourth book.

Prepare students for reading a novel by talking about the cover. Who are the characters? What do you think they're doing? Where are they? How do they feel about what's happening? Then encourage your students to just enjoy reading the story. If needed, they can take random notes to help them find details for later use, but ask them to wait with answering questions or doing activities. After reading a book through, students can return to it and glean added information to answer study questions or do other activities.

Each study guide gives you the ability to move through the questions and activities at a pace that is right for your students. Topics are organized in sections such as talking about the story, making choices, being a never-give-up family, following God's leading, discussing ideas about freedom, ideas for written or oral responses, and a digging deeper section for students who want to study further.

Your own love of reading may be one of your strongest motivators for encouraging others to read. That love and the discernment that follows will become an important gift you offer the children and young people you influence.

Whether you read these novels aloud as a group or your students read them individually, I hope that all of you enjoy them. May each of you also be blessed by growing deeper in your walk as a Freedom Seeker.

With warm regards,

Lois

Lois Walfrid Johnson

List of Characters

LIBBY NORSTAD: Tall and slender, 13 years old. Turns 14 in book #4. Just one inch shorter than Caleb who is not short. Brown eyes like her mother's, long, deep red hair with gold highlights. At beginning of first novel wears in long curls. Before time of second cover, she brushed it out with front drawn up and held by ribbon at top of head and rest of hair with slight curls at end falling down her back. Hair is wispy in front, wavy in back. First book wears full dresses and crinolines. Changes to simpler dress partway through book. Spiritually doesn't know what she believes until near the end of second book. Wants a never-give-up family. Libby's mother died 4 years before.

CAPTAIN NATHANIEL NORSTAD, LIBBY'S FATHER, PA: Captain and owner of the *Christina*. Tall, slender, brown eyes, black hair with a touch of white above the ears. Athletic movements, strong Christian, stands firm on what he believes, runs a tight ship, homeschools Libby and Caleb, then Jordan and Elsa. Norwegian. When his first wife, Christina, died, Libby was 9.

<u>CALEB WHITNEY</u>: Biblically, he stood in the right place, took the hill country even when an old man. 14 years old, almost 15. Blue eyes, blond hair falls down over his forehead, slender, but not as tall as Jordan. One inch taller than Libby. Cabin boy on *Christina*. Underground Railroad conductor since age of 9. Ardent abolitionist, wants to be a newspaper editor, strong Christian.

<u>RACHEL (GRANNY OR GRAN) WHITNEY</u>: Caleb's grandmother who has cared for him since the death of his parents from cholera. Gran is a widow and the chief pastry cook on board. Strongly antislavery, Caleb's sidekick when it comes to hiding people and she does hide them in the ship's galley when needed. Also supplies food for the hidden fugitives. Spunky, small, gray-white hair that falls out of the bun at the back of her neck. Rosy, flushed cheeks when galley hot from cooking.

<u>JORDAN PARKER</u>: African American, Black, doesn't know his birthday, about 15 or 16. Wants his birthday to be when he knows his daddy is free. Sold at estate auction in St. Louis. Muscular, strong, about 6 feet tall. Strong Christian walk, forgiving spirit, hears the Lord extraordinarily well. Singer. Good mechanic.

Father: Micah Parker

Mother: Hattie

11-year-old sister: Serena

8-year-old brother: Zack

3-year-old sister: Rose

EMMA: slave at same location in Missouri as Jordan's family, then sold farther north, along with Jordan's Momma, his brother, and two sisters. Emma's baby's name is Little Henry (rescued by Deacon Trowbridge).

AUNTIE VI THORNTON: Sister of Libby's mother, took care of Libby for four years until Libby came to live with her father. Vi lives in a mansion in Chicago.

UNCLE ALEXANDER THORNTON: Husband of Vi. Wealthy businessman.

MR. BATES: First mate, Southern sympathizer. Presses thin lips together. Thin. Almost as tall as Libby's father.

OSBORNE: Chief engineer, kind, welcoming, abolitionist

FLETCHER: *Christina*'s pilot

MARTIN: young mud clerk

MR. RIGGS: Cruel slave trader, short in height, slender around waist, wiry, wears three-piece suit that finest money can buy, carries cane with gold head that is not needed for walking. Cold blue eyes. Cruelest man Libby has ever seen. Lines between nose and outside corners of lips as though always frowning. Robert Ralph Riggs.

SLAVE CATCHERS: No name given. One blond, other light brown hair. Both tall.

HISTORIC CHARACTERS:

HARRIET TUBMAN: Moses to her people.

DR. and MRS. WILLIAM SALTER, Congregational pastor and wife in Burlington, IA.

HENDERSON LEWELLING, Amos and Ellen Kimberly and their son, Samuel: Society of Friends, owners of house in Salem, IA.

REVEREND ASA TURNER, along with Dr. Salter, part of Iowa Band that settled in southeaster corner of Iowa.

DEACON and MRS. THERON TROWBRIDGE, sheltered fugitives in their home, Deacon rescued Emma's baby.

ELIJAH LOVEJOY: First martyr for freedom of press in U. S. Killed while editor of newspaper, the *Observer*, in Alton, IL. Took anti-slavery stands.

ALL BOATS NAMED ARE HISTORIC
except for the *Christina*.

CHRISTINA: Name of the sidewheeler owned and operated by Libby's father. Steamboat is named after Libby's mother.

SAMSON: Libby's dog, a Newfoundland, better known today as a Newfie. Housebroken, but frisky when Libby gets him. Black coat with white patches on nose, muzzle, chest and tips of toes.

Acknowledgments

Often people ask me, "Lois, how can I tell who is real, and who isn't?" By that they mean, "What characters truly lived? Which characters are imaginary?" If you wonder the same thing, turn to page 6. You'll find a paragraph naming the real-life people who lived or were known during the time of this series. With each historic person I did my best to describe them as they were and according to what they did and said.

Take, for instance, Father Asa Turner, pastor of the first Congregational church in Iowa. When he saw the need for more churches, he wrote to Andover Seminary in Massachusetts and asked students to consider coming to the Iowa Territory. In response several young men gathered in the library at night, meeting in the dark to avoid the risk of fire, and praying about what they should do.

Pastor William Salter, later known as Dr. Salter, was one of those who became part of the Iowa Band. Both Father Turner and Dr. Salter provided strong spiritual and antislavery leadership during crucial years of Iowa's history.

A member of Father Turner's church, Deacon Trowbrige truly did rescue a baby from a slave owner in northeastern Missouri. The Trowbridge house still stands in Denmark,

Iowa, as a private residence. I'm grateful to Gayla Young and her daughter Stacy for showing me the secret room discovered by Gayla's grandparents, Robert and Ethel Riddle.

The Quaker community of Salem, Iowa, was a major center for the work of the Underground Railroad. Ten routes led in or out of the town. Henderson Lewelling, who built the house where the Kimberly family lived during this story, was a nurseryman who transported about 700 trees and shrubs by oxcart to Milwaukie, Oregon. There he became known as the father of the West Coast fruit industry. His brother, Seth, developed the Bing cherry.

Henderson Lewelling's home in Salem is now a museum that honors the important stand taken by members of the Society of Friends in that area. Thanks to Marcia Cammack for giving us a great tour!

And what about Elijah Lovejoy, the newspaper editor admired by Caleb? Today Mr. Lovejoy is known as the first martyr for freedom of the press in the United States. If you visit the city of Alton, Illinois, you'll find a monument to this courageous man.

The building now known as the Old Courthouse in Saint Louis has had a long and painful history. From a courtroom within those walls, Dred Scott made his first attempts to free himself from slavery.

For many years slave auctions were held on the east steps of the Old Courthouse. Then on January 1, 1861, two thousand young men gathered for the widely advertised sale of seven slaves. When the auctioneer asked for bids on the first slave, the audience roared "Three dollars!" After two hours the bidding reached eight dollars. The exhausted auctioneer finally led the slaves back to jail. Never again did someone try to sell human beings in a St. Louis auction.

In September, 1991, African Americans and whites marched side by side to the steps of the Old Courthouse. Standing in the rain, white leaders asked forgiveness for past and present sins against African Americans. Black Christians spoke out their forgiveness.

In addition to those already named, a number of other people have helped in the preparation of this book. In Denmark, Iowa, thanks to David and Peg O'Rourke, Leontina Raid, and Carol Whitmarsh.

In Alton, Illinois, thanks to Janice Wright of the visitors center; the librarians of the Hayner Public Library District; Charlene Gill, president, and Shirley Dury of the Alton Area Historical Society.

Roberta and Hurley Hagood of Hannibal, Missouri, shared generously of their time and research. My gratitude also to Susie Guest, library assistant, Burlington Free Public Library; William S. Trump Jr., pastor, and Anna Martin, historian, First Congregational Church, Burlington, Iowa; Neal Dodd and historian John Haufman of Fort Madison, Iowa; H. Scott Wolfe, historical librarian, Galena Public Library District, Galena, Illinois; Phyllis Kelley, DeKalb County historian, Sycamore, Illinois; Harry Alsman, LeClaire, Iowa; and Joseph W. Sutter, editor, *S & D Reflector*.

Emily Miller, librarian at the Missouri Historical Society Library and Collections Center, St. Louis; Barbara Kolk of the American Kennel Club Association Library, New York; Anita Taylor Doering, archivist, La Crosse Public Library; and Ed Hill, Archivist, Special Collections, Murphy Library,

University of Wisconsin, La Crosse, all gave prompt answers to my many questions.

Through the Steamer *George M. Verity* and the Keokuk River Museum at Victory Park in Keokuk, Iowa, I began to feel what it means to live on a riverboat. Robert L. Miller, curator of this National Historic Landmark, also gave of his personal knowledge and resources, helped me in countless ways, and read portions of the manuscript. A thousand thanks, Bob!

In addition to providing information, four other people also read parts of the manuscript and offered suggestions: Linda Slaikeu, Cushing, Wisconsin; Lewis Savage, Quaker pastor, Salem, Iowa; Thomas Robinson, president, Minnesota Valley Kennel Club; and Norma Robinson, president, Newfoundland Dog Club of the Greater Twin Cities, Eagan, Minnesota.

My gratitude, also, to Gene Early, Birdella Johnson, Bill Soderbeck, and Walter Johnson of Frederic, Grantsburg, and Siren, Wisconsin, and to Jena and Randy Luck of Dayton, Ohio, for help with the story line.

Sincere thanks to Bethany House for the first edition of this book and my editors Ron Klug, Barbara Lilland, and Helen Motter for their wisdom and help in developing ideas. Thanks to my artist, Andrea Jorgenson, who made Libby and the other characters come to life.

Thank you to every person at Moody Publishers who had a part in bringing out this new edition of the Freedom Seekers series: Deborah Keiser, Associate Publisher—River North, for her strong gifting, creative planning, and visionary leadership. My thanks, also, to Michele Forridor, Audience Development Manager, for day-to-day marketing and making connections with you, my audience; to Brittany Biggs, Author Relations;

and to Pam Pugh, General Project Editor, for her oversight, management, and working through the details to bring this book to completion. Thanks also to Artist Odessa Sawyer for giving us exciting art that keeps us asking, "What will happen next?"

Finally, I'm grateful to my husband, Roy. After writing a number of Northwoods novels, I asked him, "What can we do next?" When you read the student intro to the study guide you'll discover the result. Thanks, Roy, for being my terrific idea person. Thanks for the countless times you've encouraged me. And thanks for all the fun we had traveling up and down the Mississippi River while searching out the Underground Railroad.

Other Titles by Lois Walfrid Johnson

The Freedom Seekers

1. *Escape into the Night*
2. *Race for Freedom*
3. *Midnight Rescue*
4. *The Swindler's Treasure*
5. *Mysterious Signal*
6. *The Fiddler's Secret*

Adventures of the Northwoods

1. *The Disappearing Stranger*
2. *The Hidden Message*
3. *The Creeping Shadows*
4. *The Vanishing Footprints*
5. *Trouble at Wild River*
6. *The Mysterious Hideaway*
7. *Grandpa's Stolen Treasure*
8. *The Runaway Clown*
9. *Mystery of the Missing Map*
10. *Disaster on Windy Hill*

Viking Quest

1. *Raiders from the Sea*
2. *Mystery of the Silver Coins*
3. *The Invisible Friend*
4. *Heart of Courage*
5. *The Raider's Promise*

Series also available in Norwegian

FaithGirlz: *Girl Talk: 52 Weekly Devotions*

For adults: *Either Way, I Win: God's Hope for Difficult Times*

[excerpt from *Race for Freedom*]

∼ CHAPTER 1 ∼

Darker Than Night

A lantern hung near the gangplank, casting a glow over the *Christina's* deck. Libby Norstad's deep brown eyes sparkled in its light. "We got away!" she whispered to Caleb. "We really got away!"

To Libby it seemed a miracle. For the past two days and nights, they had faced constant danger.

Caleb Whitney's blond hair fell over his forehead, nearly reaching his eyes. He grinned at Libby, then glanced up at the hills of Burlington, Iowa. The steamboat owned by Libby's father lay at the landing. While deckhands brought in the gangplank, Caleb kept watch.

Now, late at night, the streets looked empty, yet Libby knew that Caleb was searching for someone. Near the riverfront, the windows of tall warehouses seemed like dark eyes staring down at them.

With three quick blasts of the whistle, the *Christina* put out into the Mississippi River. As the strip of water between the land and boat grew wide, Libby felt relieved. In spite of all kinds of danger, they had escaped!

Just then Libby felt a movement behind her. As she turned, she saw Jordan Parker creeping forward without a sound.

When he drew close to the lantern, he stopped, as if afraid to enter the circle of light.

A fugitive slave, Jordan had managed to get away from his master, a cruel slave trader named Riggs. Like Caleb, Jordan also stared up at the city. On the streets above them no one stirred. Then a dark shape stepped out from the shadow of a warehouse.

Jordan moaned. "It's Riggs!"

With one quick movement, Caleb lifted the glass of the lantern and blew out the flame. Libby dropped down on her hands and knees, but it was too late.

"Riggs knows," she whispered as Caleb joined her behind piles of freight. "He saw you."

"He saw you too," Caleb warned, his voice low.

A feeling of dread tightened Libby's stomach. "What should we do?"

Caleb shushed her. "Sound carries on water."

A short distance out from shore, the *Christina* started to turn. As her bow swung around to face downstream, Libby stared at the man next to the warehouse. Then the center of the boat blocked her view.

"How long was Riggs there?" she whispered. "How much did he see?"

"Too much," Caleb told her. At fourteen, almost fifteen, he was nearly a year older than Libby. Now Caleb led her and Jordan to a place at the front of the boat where no one could hear them talk.

When the boys dropped down on crates, Libby found a nail keg to sit on. "You're sure it was Riggs?" she asked. It had been too dark to see the man's face, and she wanted to believe they were wrong. According to Caleb, Riggs was the cruelest man he knew.

"It were Riggs, all right." Jordan's voice held no doubt. "He gots one shape—and I knows it!"

"But he could have stayed hidden," Libby answered. "Why did he step out so we could see him?"

"That man *wants* us to know he's on our trail," Jordan said. "He wants to scare us any way he can."

In the darkness Libby shivered. As long as the slave trader searched for him, Jordan would never be safe. Libby didn't like being frightened by the sight of Riggs, but deep inside she trembled just thinking about him.

Then she remembered. "Jordan, you weren't in the light. Maybe Riggs doesn't know that you're with us."

Jordan sighed. "I wish you was right, Libby. That man Riggs is like a bloodhound on my trail. When he sniffs out Caleb, he sniffs out me."

Since the age of nine, Caleb had worked on the Underground Railroad, the secret plan to help runaway slaves reach freedom. Once fugitives started on the secret route, they usually kept moving if it was safe. Instead, for special reasons, Jordan would stay on the *Christina*.

"What's wrong?" Caleb asked Libby, as though sensing her worry.

"N–n–nothing!" Libby hated the sound of her voice. "Nothing at all!" If she told Caleb what bothered her, he would think she was a scaredy-cat. Instead, Libby tried to push her fear away. *I want to have courage*, she thought. *Courage like Caleb and Jordan.*

On that March night in 1857, Libby knew the penalty for anyone who helped runaway slaves on their race to freedom.

According to law, slave hunters could follow fugitives into free states. There they could gather a posse and bring runaways back to their owners.

Leaning closer, Caleb peered into Libby's face. When she tried to hide her feelings, the light of the moon gave her away. "You're scared," Caleb said. "You're scared that Riggs will come on board and find Jordan."

"Well, doesn't that frighten you?" Libby asked.

"Nope," Caleb answered.

"What do you mean, *nope*? Pa is captain of this boat and owner too. Don't you care that he could be arrested for hiding a runaway slave?"

"Of course I care!"

"You don't sound like it!" Libby felt upset now. "You know what would happen if Riggs found Jordan on the *Christina*. It's the law of the land that Pa could be found guilty for hiding a fugitive. He'd have to pay a big fine!"

"Is that all you're worried about?" Caleb asked. "The fines? The money?"

Libby stared at him. "What if Pa can't pay the fines? He would lose the *Christina*!"

"Yup! He would." Caleb didn't sound too upset.

"What's worse, Pa could go to jail! Wouldn't you be scared if the captain were your father?"

Caleb sat with his back to the moon. Darkness shadowed his face, but Libby saw the shake of his head. "There's something that bothers me a whole lot more," he said.

"What's that?" Libby asked. More than once she had found it hard to understand this strange boy. "What could be worse than Pa going to jail?"

Before Caleb could answer, Jordan leaped up. "Don't you worry none," he told Libby. "First stop we make, I leaves the boat."

"No!" Caleb exclaimed. "Don't listen to Libby! You can't leave now!"

"Yes, I can. I ain't goin' to hurt Libby's Pa."

"That's true," Caleb answered. "You aren't going to hurt Captain Norstad."

"But you heard Libby."

"Yup, I heard." Caleb sounded angry. "And I won't let you hurt her pa. I'll keep hiding you for as long as you need to be hid."

Jordan shook his bowed head. "I was wrong to ask Captain Norstad if I could stay."

"He gave his permission," Caleb answered. "Remember?"

"I remembers. And he gave me a job." Jordan's shoulders shifted as though the idea of working for pay gave him pleasure.

"Don't forget the reason Captain Norstad said you could stay."

Jordan straightened. "'Cause I wants to find my daddy. I wants to be my momma's hands. Momma is mighty strong. But if she runs away, she ain't got enough hands for my sisters and my brother."

In the moonlight Jordan stood sure and tall. "Momma don't know if I is dead or alive. She be moanin' and weepin' for me, and here I is—free as a bird from a cage!"

For the first time since seeing Riggs, Jordan's gaze met Caleb's. "When I leaves this boat, I is goin' to the place where Momma lives. I is goin' to help my momma and my sisters and my brother escape!"

"You want to go there *now*?" Caleb stared at Jordan. "You can't do that! On every tree and building, there are posters about you! Every slave catcher on earth wants to collect that big reward!"

But Jordan was wearing his proud look—the look that reminded Libby of royalty. With his head high, he spoke. "When I was just a little boy, my momma told me, 'Jordan, you is goin' to lead your people to the Promised Land. You is goin' to take them to *freedom*!'"

"That's right," Caleb answered. "You *will* lead your people to freedom! But if you try now, you'll lose *your* freedom."

When Jordan blinked, Caleb rushed on. "Have you got a plan figured out? Do you know a way to disguise who you are?"

Jordan shook his head.

"Do you know how to get to where your mother is?"

Again Jordan shook his head. "I ain't never seen where Momma lives now. When I gits there, I'll know what to do."

"Then let's think of a way you can get there without being caught," Caleb said.

Looking as though he didn't want to listen, Jordan dropped back down on a crate. "We gots to figure out that plan real soon," he said. "I ain't goin' to wait for something more to happen to Momma."

As if Libby were no longer there, Caleb leaned forward, speaking to Jordan. "I want to help you find every member of your family. You tell me what to do, and I'll do it."

"I tell *you* what to do?" Again Jordan leaped to his feet. This time his eyes blazed. "You is foolin' me, sure enough! There ain't no slave boy who tells a white boy what to do!"

"I know what to do if I find a runaway slave," Caleb said.

"I know how to hide a fugitive who comes near the *Christina*. What you need to do will be a whole lot harder."

Standing as still as a stone, Jordan seemed to consider Caleb's words. Finally he turned. "You thinks I can lead my people to freedom?"

Caleb's gaze held steady. "I *know* you can lead your people to freedom. If you'd like my help, you've got it." As though wanting to shake on it, Caleb offered his hand.

Jordan stared down at Caleb's hand, then looked up. "You *really* wants to help me?" he asked.

"I really want to help you," Caleb said.

As if he had never before touched a white boy's hand, Jordan hesitated. Then, seeming to make up his mind, he stretched out his own hand. Halfway between the two boys, their hands met.

Jordan grinned. "I hope you knows what you is doing."

"First, we keep you safe," Caleb promised. "Then we figure out a way to get to your family."

In that moment Libby felt scared right down to her toes. Something important had been decided. Something that would change Jordan's life but also Caleb's and hers. Even the thought of what might happen frightened Libby.

I wish I had their courage, she told herself again. Then she remembered the man on the Burlington street. It had been too dark to see the evil lines in his face. Yet a shiver of fear ran through Libby—a shiver so strong that she trembled.

With all her heart, she wanted Jordan's mother and sisters and brother to reach freedom. With all her heart, she wanted Jordan to find the father who had been sold away from the family. But Libby knew how dangerous it would be.

One idea haunted her. *How can we hide from Riggs wherever we go?*

As if knowing her thoughts, Caleb spoke. "We can be sure of one thing. Riggs will do everything he can to stop us. Wherever we are, he won't be far behind!"